Killing a Mouse
on Sunday

A beautifully told, supremely human story,
hovering between humour and tragedy, by
the author and producer of *The Life and
Death of Colonel Blimp*, *The Red Shoes* and
other memorable films.

To the French authorities, Manuel Artiguez
is just one of thousands of exiled Spaniards
living in Pau. But across the wild Pyrenees,
in Spain, he is known as an audacious and
dangerous bandit with a 100,000-peseta price
on his head, who for the past twenty years
has been harassing the Spanish authorities
and official institutions. To Captain Viñolas,
chief of the Pamplona police, his capture has
become an obsession.

With the arrival in Pau of a small Spanish
boy and of Father Francisco, a devout young
priest on his way to a pilgrimage to Lourdes,
this twenty-year drama comes to a thrilling
and moving climax, in the course of which
both priest and outlaw come to a new understanding of some of the simple values of life.

EMERIC PRESSBURGER

KILLING A MOUSE ON SUNDAY

Drawings by Papas

THE REPRINT SOCIETY LTD.
LONDON

FIRST PUBLISHED 1961
THIS EDITION PUBLISHED BY THE REPRINT SOCIETY LTD.
BY ARRANGEMENT WITH WM. COLLINS SONS & CO. LTD.
1963

To My Friend, Stapi

. . . I saw a Puritane-one
Hanging of his cat on Monday,
For killing of a mouse on Sunday.

RICHARD BRATHWAITE *(d.* 1673)

I

WE HAD BEEN CLIMBING ever since midnight, my father's second cousin and I. Since he could whistle beautifully, everybody called him "The Flute" except myself. I tried once, about three months ago, when Father, he and I went fishing, but Father said I mustn't call him "The Flute", for it sounded disrespectful for a boy of eleven to call a man of sixty-five anything but Uncle Luis.

We climbed in silence which did not bother me, but I knew it must be bothering Uncle Luis, for he loved to whistle when climbing. We had not rested for more than an hour, the last time when we reached the forest. He puffed like a railway engine and I puffed too and he asked me whether I wanted to sit down, but I told him that I was playing trains to pass away the time. He stopped all the same for he had got so tired that he couldn't even puff any more. He asked me if I knew where we had got to and I told him that we were near the woodcutter's hut from which you could see the waterfall and where I once saw a bear while collecting wild strawberries. Everybody said it couldn't be true, no one has ever seen a bear in these parts, but Father declared that he, for one, believed me for I had eyes like a hawk and somebody said I had a nose, too, like a hawk and everybody laughed except my father and, of course, myself.

Uncle Luis spoke very softly, stopping now and then to listen for sounds he attributed to border patrols. The sounds were nothing but a hare woken up by us, now lying in its burrow, holding its breath, waiting for a chance to scurry as silently as it could, to another hiding place. Or a bird dreaming, losing balance on the branch of a tree. Or a branch moving in the breeze. My father wouldn't be afraid of birds and branches. He wouldn't be afraid of anything except, perhaps, Captain Viñolas himself. No, not even of Viñolas. Not of him and not of the whole Pamplona police. They had tortured him and he didn't name any of his friends who kept contact with the Spanish refugees in France.

" I hope you'll never forget your father," Uncle Luis said, as if I could ever forget him. Then I thought perhaps it is much more difficult to remember after all, for I have almost forgotten my mother. I couldn't recollect more than a beautiful shape, dark in her black dress, the olive skin under her raven tresses, the two burning candles and the shame of a priest coming to pray at the funeral, people asking questions about the priest and my father explaining that she had never given up her religion and that, in her death, he respected her wish to have a funeral with a priest, bells tolling, a funeral-sermon and a wooden cross over the grave.

" And I hope you'll never forget those brutes who killed him," added Uncle Luis.

I could promise that. I stood for many days in front of the police station while they had my father there. I could remember Viñolas the chief butcher, and the lesser butchers—every single one of them. And after my father died I used to lay in wait for Viñolas, close to his house, watching him coming home or going out in his car. The face of every sentry of the guardia civil who had ever stood guard at Viñolas's home was engraved in my brain.

We climbed for another half an hour among the tall dark trees. It reminded me of a painting I made in school of a company of soldiers, all huge men standing erect, and in front of them stood a little fat general, bandy-legged, with bloated stomach, and the teacher made me overpaint it with black ink, but you could always see the shapes of the soldiers and the misbegotten little fellow; no black ink could obliterate them, just like the night could not obliterate the shapes of the trees.

I have always thought that the frontier ran on the highest ridge of the mountain, but Uncle Luis said it was stupid. The border between countries depended solely on the fancy of capitalists. In those days when boundary lines were carved out, Uncle Luis said, the dukes and barons of two countries met and one said, I'll keep this mountain because my dogs like to hunt here, you can have that valley in exchange. And so they carved up the place, not giving a hoot what the poor people of the district suffered, splitting families, leaving a village without pasturage, houses without a road, men and beasts without water.

At long last we got to the top of the ridge. To the right, over the trees, a dark green line appeared in the sky, it got thicker every minute.

" We must hurry," said Uncle Luis, and panted faster as we stumbled down the slope. He stopped and held my arm. From below came the purr of a brook, it might be the Verderiz, I thought. I have never been as far as that, but my father used to tell me about it when he took me along to watch him catching the trout. I loved to scan the water for little silver lightnings, accompanied by mighty splashes as the trout played or fought in the green morning.

" It's called the Verderiz," Uncle Luis whispered. " The other side is France."

What a terrible let-down it was! There were the same trees, the same grass, the same sky. The wind played the same tune among the leaves high up in the foliage. I thought, it should be a French tune which I couldn't understand, something I had never heard before. I saw many French posters of pretty girls, scantily dressed in a way Viñolas's policemen would never tolerate in Pamplona. Once they had arrested two young women who were sun-bathing on a hotel balcony with almost nothing on. A boy in school brought a newspaper and read it out and we all had been thrilled by it and gloated at the photograph which could have been anything, for the printer's ink had run amok over it. And it said that they were French girls who had come to Pamplona for a holiday, and the paper said that if they behaved like that, they could just as well stay at home in France.

Uncle Luis insisted it was France on the other side. He should know. He went over many times, nobody knew exactly what he did there, but the boys were sure that

Uncle Luis smuggled Spanish banknotes to France, and coffee and tea from there back to Spain. Everybody regarded him as an expert on French affairs and I listened carefully, so that I wouldn't miss anything.

"Walk downhill all the time. Don't run, running is noisy. After a while you'll get to the road. Turn left and stay in the forest. Don't walk on the road. Walk under the trees."

I asked him what to do about the French police. He spat into the Verderiz.

"If you see them, stop. They ride on bicycles. Always two of them. They smoke and talk of women. They won't spot you."

I was glad about that. I would have hated to be stopped by any police. Especially by the French. I wouldn't understand what they asked me. We learnt French in school, but who has ever heard of learning a foreign language in school? My father used to say: "You can't learn even your own language in school." What an understanding man my father was!

Uncle Luis was not finished yet. Not by a long chalk. He told me to walk along the road for about half an hour, until I found a bridge. Then I was to turn right for a change, into a narrow lane, and walk again. Not very long this time. Only about three minutes—until I saw a white Basque house with green timber and roses in the front garden. This house belonged to Pedro, a friend of my father.

"Tell him you're Pablo Dages, José Dages's son. He'll see to it that you get to Pau and find your Uncle Antonio there. Tell Pedro all there is to tell."

Uncle Luis was waiting. I could see it in the way he stood there under the tree, waiting for me to go so that he, too, could go back up the ridge and then down to Elizondo, where he would take the bus to Pamplona. In Elizondo he would go to the grocer and pick up his wine-skin which he left there last night so that he didn't have to burden himself with the weight of it. I heard him telling the grocer to fill it up with red wine and he would have to fill it again before the bus left. I said good-bye to the grocer and he did not ask where I was going, or when I should come back again. People in Elizondo never asked questions, not such questions anyway.

I suppose Uncle Luis waited for me to say good-bye now. I was quite good at bidding good-bye these days, for I had done nothing lately but bid good-bye. I shook hands with the boys at school, with those that is whom one could trust. I trusted only one teacher out of the lot, he taught geography and liked me because I was good at geography. I went up to him and said, " Good night, sir," and held out my hand and he knew at once what it meant: that I would not come to school to-morrow, or the day after, or ever. People in Pamplona were used to saying good night, knowing that it means perhaps farewell for many years. When the workmen struck in the locomotive factory, many had to cross the border. After every strike there were many good nights which meant good-bye.

Uncle Luis waited, but I couldn't go just yet. In his right trouser-pocket, rolled into a knotted handkerchief, he held the Thing and I couldn't leave without it. I would rather die. He opened his arms and embraced me and I could smell sour wine in his clothes and his pipe-smoky breath.

While he held me in his arms, I was watching the brook. I saw a trout cruising lazily. And another and a third,

and kept on smelling the sour wine and the smoky breath
until his strong arms loosened their grip and I was free
once more.

"What are you waiting for?" he asked. I wished he
hadn't. I hoped he would remember without my reminding
him.

"You have forgotten the watch. My father's watch . . .
you told me you'd give it to me before I went."

"So I did. What a memory you have, Pablo. A small
boy doesn't need a watch. But I *do*. I have to check the
time all day. With the job I'm doing."

I didn't know what job he was referring to, and I knew
he didn't like me mentioning the watch. All the same, he
took the knotted handkerchief from his trouser-pocket,
untied it, and handed the watch to me. It did not gleam as
it used to when Father had it and it had stopped going.

I could make it shine again and I would as soon as I got
away.

"Keep it in your pocket," he said. "It's too big for
your wrist." He knew that I saw the little golden cross in
the handkerchief. "You don't want this."

"I do," I pleaded.

"You don't believe in that nonsense of churches, priests,
crosses, and such-like, do you?"

I didn't. But this was a special cross, my mother used
to wear it around her neck. Uncle Luis was determined to
keep it and I was determined to get it.

"You don't want to carry a cross in your pocket. It's
unlucky."

I told him that my father had carried it in his pocket
ever since my mother died, but Uncle Luis reminded me
that it hadn't brought him much luck either. It occurred to
me that if it was so unlucky, he should be glad to be rid
of it, but he probably wanted to sell it and buy something
useful with the money—like a skinful of wine. He must
have thought of wine himself, for he swallowed several
times as men do when their throats are dry. He gave me
the cross with an air of doom.

"There, now you've got your whole inheritance. Ask
someone in Pau to melt it down for you. And don't show
it round in the Spanish Street, or people will think you're
religious."

That made sense. I promised to be careful about it and
put the watch and the gold cross in my pocket. He stood
there while I jumped over the brook and the trout flashed
in silver lightnings in all directions. When I turned, I saw
him climbing towards the ridge. He must be glad that it
was over and soon he would start whistling for he had
nothing to hide any more, even if he met some carabineros.

I turned again, but he had disappeared, the billowing trees had swallowed him up. I stopped to look at my watch. I wound it and it started going straight away. It needed only a little rubbing and it shone like real silver. Perhaps it *was* silver. I tried it on my wrist. The Flute was wrong, one could see that the strap was the right size—my wrist was too small.

I skipped down the slope, deeper and deeper into France. Once I could hear voices, the mooing of cows, the bell of a bicycle, a dog barking. I scouted forward on the soft turf, now on level ground, and there above some hazelnut bushes, floated two fat men in uniform, cigarettes dangling from their mouths, talking in their foreign tongue.

The shepherd stood in the middle of the road, waiting for the herd to cross. His dog did the work, urging the cows to hurry. The man just stood, red-faced from the rising sun, looking up at two parallel vapour-trails at the ends of which tiny specks bore through the sky. Being aware of them made one hear them, too, a faint high-pitched hum of jet planes, probably from the aerodrome at Valladolid. And then I remembered that I was in France, the trees were French and so were the cows and the planes and they came perhaps from Toulouse, or Paris, or Lyons, and I also thought of learning geography in French and perhaps my uncle in Pau would want to send me to a French school and I couldn't speak a word of French. Or they might have a Spanish school in Pau, after all they had a Spanish street and in Toulouse they had even a Spanish newspaper, which proved that we Spaniards were more important people than the French, since there were no French newspapers in Pamplona or in Irun, and no French streets either.

Suddenly the forest ended. The Flute never told me that it would. In the distance I could see a line of trees

which could be the river. There had to be a river or
something if there was a bridge, and I had to find that
bridge, so that I could cross it and take the lane to the
right. I decided to walk on the road against the warning
of The Flute. There was little choice and a boy walking
on a road looked less conspicuous than crossing fields of
wheat. It was a fine road, wide and clean, no animal-
droppings on it as in Spain. You couldn't see a single
donkey as far as the eye could reach, only a bright red
tractor crossing the bridge. On the bridge there was a
sign which said " Aldudes ". On the other side another,
with the same word written on it. Did the French call
their bridges by names, or was it the name of the river?
If it was supposed to be the name of a river, it did not
deserve a name, for I could discover no water under the
bridge, just cracked hard mud. I turned into the lane,
passing several houses, some of them had cars parked in
front of them, all seemed new cars, makes I had never seen
before. I stopped to admire one with a complicated dash-
board, dials and clocks and switches. In the silence I could
hear the clock ticking and it showed five minutes to five
and I adjusted my watch to the time.

I found Pedro's house without difficulty. It had the
roses and the green timbers and though many houses grew
roses, most of them had rusty-coloured timbers, or no
timbers at all.

I couldn't disturb them so early, and so I settled down in
front of Pedro's house to wait for a sign that they were up.
I watched the swallows flying high which meant that the
weather would be good for days. A few minutes later a car
came from the bridge. It drove fast, the owner, a young
man, stared surprised at me, turning around several times
and almost hitting a telegraph pole. Often I consulted

my watch dangling from my wrist. It showed five-fifteen, then five-sixteen and then five-seventeen. At five-twenty-two, somebody opened the green shutters and a woman in a night-shirt called back into the room:

" There's a boy outside! "

She spoke Spanish. A second later, a short man of my father's age, joined her at the window. He, too, had a night-shirt on. He had a kind face, a lean body and an unlit pipe in his hand.

" Look who's here! " he greeted me. He disappeared from the window, leaving the hard-faced woman staring at me. I smiled at her, but she kept on staring without a trace of friendliness, then Pedro opened the door and came out into the little garden at the front of the house. He had slipped a pair of trousers on, and was now tucking his night-shirt into them while he opened the tiny gate under the roses.

" You must be José Dages's son." He held out his hand and I shook it.

" What's your name? "

There was the sunshine of friendliness in his voice and the ray of fun in his eyes. I liked him at once. He reminded me very much of my father, though they were very different in looks: my father measured almost two metres, while Pedro couldn't be much more than one fifty-five. Pedro had little hair, while my father had kept his black mane right to the end, but they had the same grin, disguised under serious eyebrows, visible only to those for whom it was meant. The Flute told me once that my father was a rascal. And so was Pedro. We went inside and the silent woman made breakfast and stood behind us while we men gulped it down in the Basque fashion. I never knew that Pedro was a Basque and it did not matter. He was a rascal and great fun.

After breakfast while the silent woman washed the dishes, I had to tell Pedro how things had happened to my father. How, first, Lieutenant Zapater called and searched our flat but couldn't find anything. My father was out, he went to burn some papers in the big furnace of the factory where he worked as a week-end caretaker and from whence he never returned. They questioned me about the people who used to come to us; Zapater asked me if I knew Manuel Artiguez? I told him that I had heard of him and he wanted to know whether I thought that Manuel was a bad man or a good one, and I told him that he must be very bad since the police were looking for him and the newspapers called him the greatest bandit of the century. Zapater asked me if I remembered the day when Manuel raided the church in Pamplona two years ago, and whether my father ever talked about it, and I said we talked about it as everybody else did, and he asked if I would denounce Manuel if he ever came to our flat, and I said I wouldn't because he would kill me and he would kill my father. What worried him more than anything was to find out whom we knew among the Spanish exiles in France; he said he knew for sure that we had friends there and that my father sent messages to them.

Pedro nodded several times.

" The work of a traitor," he said. " There must be somebody who knows a lot about what's going on."

Later he brought out a large box full of photographs and showed me some with my father in them. They were taken in the civil war and my father looked young and dashing. In one, he stood with Pedro and a fierce-looking fellow and Pedro said that was Manuel Artiguez himself. I never saw Manuel's photograph as a young fighter as we had burned all our photographs a long time ago. It was dangerous to keep such pictures in Spain and nobody had them. I asked Pedro if he had ever met the great Manuel Artiguez and he laughed and told me, with a grin, that he took part in that famous raid two years ago and in many others before. I asked him if he would join Manuel again and he shook his head and did not grin this time.

Pedro did nothing the whole blessed day. We just talked about my father and we talked also about Manuel Artiguez. Through Pedro, who knew many stories of Manuel, I felt that I got to know him too. He said that one day when he came to Pau he would take me to Manuel and introduce me to him. He did not like meeting people these days but he would not mind meeting me since I was José Dages's son.

We went to a bar, which they call a bistro here, and Pedro introduced me to other men and all of them knew of my father and asked questions and made me drink red wine, but no one drank wine from skins. They poured it out into glasses, just like water, and you didn't have the pure taste of nothing-but-wine as when you squeezed the skin and it squirted into your mouth without the taste of thick glass, and I hated the marks on the glasses and often flies got into them and people spat them out as if nothing had happened.

The silent woman cooked lunch and Pedro and I and two other men ate huge portions of *paella* while she stood behind us, serving. I wondered when she had her food, for I had never seen her eating. At six p.m. the cows came home and I wondered if they belonged to the same herd

I had seen this morning and I asked Pedro and he said they
did. The silent woman milked them and started to prepare
dinner. Pedro and I walked over to the bistro again and
when we came back I couldn't go to the bathroom since
the silent woman was having a bath. Pedro suggested we
go back to the bistro which had a fine lavatory. Pedro
wanted me to go to bed early because he knew I had had
no sleep last night. Next morning he would take me to
St. Etienne-de-Baigorry, where he had a friend who went
twice weekly to fetch wine from Pau and could take me
there and deliver me to my uncle, Antonio. Pedro had little
to say about my uncle who worked as a foreman in a furniture factory and though he was my father's brother, never
excelled in the civil war. He could have stayed in Spain
but for being the brother of my father who had made
for himself a great name as a fighter. As it happened, my
father could not leave because of his chest wound; he
stayed on, served a short sentence, got an amnesty, not
because they trusted him but because they needed the
prisons for other people. In the end he stayed on, saying
that one needed good Spaniards also in Spain. Antonio
was what Lieutenant Zapater would call a good man.
Pedro told me that he married a French woman who learnt
Spanish and who would sit with him at table and sometimes
cooked and sometimes didn't, and they did not live in the
Spanish Street, but some little distance from it, though not
too far. I could easily go there to play with the other boys.
He said Manuel Artiguez lived there and I wanted to go
there to play so that one day I might see him and, perhaps,
he would drop something and I could pick it up for him
and he might look at me and say that I resembled a good
fighter called José Dages, and I would tell him that my
name was Pablo Dages and that my father was tortured

and killed by Viñolas and his butchers and Manuel would promise to avenge my father and go over to Spain and shoot Viñolas and Lieutenant Zapater, together with a dozen carabineros and soldiers and another dozen guardia civil.

I couldn't sleep and heard a clock striking the " three ones " which I always wanted to hear, but never did, for however hard I tried to stay awake, I always fell asleep. I think Pepito, The Bicycle, was the first who told me about the secret of the " three ones ", the only time at night when the clocks struck only once three times in a row, at half-hourly intervals : at half past midnight, at one o'clock and at one-thirty. It was lucky to hear the " three ones ", but it had to be at night, during day-time it meant nothing. Here, in Pedro's house, I heard them for the first time in my life. So I felt very pleased with myself and decided to write a letter to The Bicycle, who was so called on account of his limping, but I changed my mind since my letter could be opened by Viñolas's police and get The Bicycle into trouble. Anyway, I fell asleep soon after.

Pedro had a car, called a Renault, with the engine in the back. We had much coffee and smoked ham before we started and the silent woman gave me a huge parcel of sandwiches and coffee in a green bottle with a porcelain cork on hinges attached to the neck of the bottle and there was a sort of rubber washer on the porcelain cork which made the coffee smell like a hot-water bottle which I used to smell in the hospital when they allowed me to visit my father before he died.

The silent woman kissed me, she even smiled a little, but had not much time for smiling for she had to feed her chickens and ducks, which made a lot of noise, and Pedro said :

"Your ducks want you!" And she went, looking back twice as Pedro shook his head and confided in me: "She's crazy about children but can't have one."

Pedro drove in the French fashion, fast, hooting a lot and cursing everybody who overtook him, or who did not slow down when he wanted to overtake. It took only twenty minutes to get to St. Etienne-de-Baigorry, but I heard no one speaking Spanish. It worried me not being able to understand the language and it worried me more when I met the man who was to take me to Pau, for he couldn't speak a single word of Spanish and Pedro explained everything to him in Basque and it sounded to me like gibberish in a foreign tongue, for if you talked gibberish in Spanish, you could understand occasional words, but here you couldn't. Pedro called the man Marcel, told him that I couldn't speak French and explained where my uncle lived in Pau and it took a very long time, since Pedro didn't remember the name of the street. But luckily he remembered two things which, like latitude and longitude defined beyond any doubt the exact geographical position of a place on the map, would determine the exact situation of Antonio's home. One was a bistro, called Le Navarre, the other the name of his French wife, Monique. Being a man of wines, Marcel had heard of Le Navarre and, being a Frenchman who liked women whatever their name, he was certain to find her. All this Pedro had translated to me and then they started to talk about Pelota Basque and Pedro translated every word of the information he got from Marcel on the pelota championships of the Pyrenees which started to-day here in St. Etienne. Pedro decided to stay and watch to-night's games and Marcel had so much understanding for this that he, too, examined the possibilities of postponing his trip to Pau. Finally, Marcel's wife appeared, bringing a long list of things she wanted her husband to bring back from the city, Marcel got into the car, Pedro grinned his most rascally grin and, with much hooting and much mock bawling at the people standing about on the square, people all of whom seemed to be Marcel's friends, we careered down the road.

Though he well knew that I couldn't understand his language, he kept on talking to me, explaining the landscape, making funny remarks about the girls we passed—I imagined they were funny since Marcel laughed a lot when he made them. He had a Citroën van, a new model with a tremendous hooter. Each time he lit a cigarette, he gave me the wheel and as he smoked continuously, I drove almost as much as he did. At Oloron we stopped for lunch. We ate in the garden on the bank of a river called Gave d'Ossau. Marcel knew the owner, who spoke a few words of Spanish, and he explained to me that he made all sorts of ornaments of piano-wire, and brought out a lot of them to show me: candlesticks, fruit bowls, salad bowls, flower bowls, in fact every kind of bowl under the sun. Marcel inquired from the owner's wife whether he took out all the wires from their piano. I understood this because I saw Marcel opening the bowels of the piano in the inside room when he came back from the toilet, and the owner pushed one of his bowls down on Marcel's head like a hat which made an awful mess of Marcel's well-groomed hair, making him a little angry. But the owner brought a bottle of very good wine and uncorked it as a peace-offering, inviting other guests as well to join in. There were four more tables occupied, one by a very large family consisting of four children, an elderly woman and the children's parents, the man fat, with a little moustache, the woman enormously pregnant, rather pretty, suffering from the midday heat. The husband talked to a pretty young waitress and a minute later she and the owner brought out a field-bed with a mattress on it. I thought it most considerate of the husband with the moustache, but as soon as they had finished setting up the bed, it was he who lay down on it. The pregnant woman took off her shoes, waded into the water and collected all the children around her so that they would let papa rest.

From here it took us less than half an hour to get to Pau. We found the bistro, Le Navarre, the innkeeper had no idea who my uncle was but as soon as Marcel mentioned something about being Spanish, the waiter scratched his head and a glimmer of hope appeared in one of his eyes. The other eye was bloodshot and full of tears and he kept on rubbing it. I suppose something had flown into it, a wine-fly, or a piece of grit, because Marcel had taken a good look at it and given him some advice on how to get it out, whatever it was. Anyway, the waiter stopped a passer-by, a pretty woman who wore a tight skirt and a sleeveless blouse with practically no back to it, the sort the police would never tolerate in Pamplona. She knew my uncle and pointed out the house where he lived. She, too, had a look at the waiter's bad eye, and then Marcel and I got on our way.

The house had four floors. Antonio's flat was on the third. My French aunt opened the door. She knew at once who I was and seemed terribly pleased to see me. She spoke quite good Spanish with a French accent, but I did not mind, I rather liked her. She asked me where my things were and when I told her that I had no things, she laughed with gleaming white teeth, and offered a glass of

wine to Marcel and she poured out one glass for me, too.
Marcel said it was Jurançon wine and when he took the
bottle from her to prove it, he held her hand on the bottle
for a moment and she gave him a severe look. He held
out a packet of cigarettes, she took one and when he lit it,
he again touched her hand and she didn't mind this time.
I had never seen a woman smoking at home before. Of
course, many smoked in the cafés in Pamplona, too, I saw
them last year when The Bicycle and I were collecting
bottle-tops and we used to stand about near the cafés
watching what the people ordered and when the waiter
had brought a bottle of something, we descended upon it
as soon as the waiter had gone and asked politely to be
allowed to take the metal tops. I had a small bag to keep
them in and at the end of a really good day I had more than
a hundred. I wondered who got them now? Perhaps
Lieutenant Zapater had a boy who collected bottle-tops, or
The Flute had taken them hoping to sell the lot and buy
red wine with the money, though I didn't think there was
much market or I might have sold them myself.

Marcel left. I had thanked him for the ride and the
lunch and he said he would come to see me from time to
time and when he said it, he didn't look at me but at my
French aunt. After he went, she showed me a little room
and said that it was mine. She laughed at my surprise and
couldn't believe that I had never had a room of my own,
not even when my mother was still alive. I used to sleep
with my parents in the same room. She thought it odd and
asked if my parents never wanted to be alone. I couldn't
answer that one for I couldn't remember.

Around six o'clock my uncle arrived. He looked like
my father in many ways but in many others he was different.
I could see that he would never make a good fighter. He

asked me about school and told me that I would start going
to school in September, till then I would learn some French.
He asked my French aunt not to talk much to me in Spanish
and she laughed, showing her beautiful teeth and promised.

" I'll make a good man of you, Pablo," he said and
I wondered what he meant. " Don't go to the Spanish
Street if you can help it. It's full of little rascals and you'll
never learn the language if you speak Spanish all the time."

I wondered what he meant by " rascals ". My father
was a rascal and so was Pedro. I had no wish to become the
sort of " good man " Lieutenant Zapater talked about.

" To-morrow we'll go to the police," he went on and
when I started to hiccup and explained that I always hic-
cupped when I got excited, he gave his reasons. " One of
these days you will want to get a French passport. It's
better they should find out who you are now, while you're
a child, than later. You don't want to live as two hundred
thousand exiles do, waiting for the day when things change
in Spain. Some have been waiting since '37, almost a
quarter of a century."

" I don't want to be French," I said. " I want to remain
Spanish."

My French aunt laughed and I was sorry to have said it.

" Do you think your uncle has become French? O-là-là!
To get a French passport doesn't make you French."

We had dinner at eight. She cooked it in no time. I
thought of the Silent Woman in Pedro's house who started
to cook dinner as soon as she had washed up the dishes
from lunch. This food was just as good and it took my
aunt only ten minutes to prepare. She sliced some veal,
dipped the slices in flour and then into sizzling hot fat.
She got a bag of frozen peas from the ice-box, in two

minutes they were boiling. She got the wine out. Antonio poured some into her glass.

"Who's been drinking Jurançon?" he asked.

She laughed. "Pablo and I. Do you mind?"

She looked at me and we had a secret. Not a big secret, but it was a secret all the same.

There were four rooms and the kitchen, and the bathroom, all opening from the passage. At the end of the passage was the toilet. She gave me a pyjama-top which belonged to Antonio, but the sleeves were longer than the legs of my trousers. She held it in front of me and when Antonio observed that it would do for one night, she disagreed and brought one of her own pyjama-tops. The sleeves fitted me nicely and it felt warm and soft and smelt a little scented and when I went to bed it seemed that I wasn't alone under the sheets and I took it off, but that didn't seem right either. I laid it beside me, under the blanket. I couldn't sleep. I heard the " three ones " again and then I had to get up to go to the toilet. Now it seemed stupid not to have used the toilet when Antonio asked me. I put on my trousers in the dark, not switching on the light for fear of waking them up, and I was glad at being so good at geography since I remembered where the toilet lay perfectly. My door creaked and the floorboards in the passage creaked, too. I tried to find the light switch in the toilet, but I couldn't. I opened the door again to see better and found that the passage had enough reflected light to find my way about. Still, I couldn't well leave the door open. What if somebody came out of their bedroom? If my uncle wanted a glass of water from the kitchen? Or —I fainted at the thought—if my French aunt came out and saw me! The door *had* to be closed. I examined the narrow walls, inside and outside, there was no switch. I saw the bulb on the ceiling, but no switch. Being a shy boy, there was no question of what I had to do. I took a good look at everything, closed the door, and turned the fastening ring. The light went on like magic.

On clear days, Pau had a lovely view of the mountains. You could see several ranges, one above and beyond the others, the farthest still had snow on it although we were in June. On Sunday we went promenading on the Boulevard des Pyrénées. When my aunt saw how interested I was in the funicular, she asked Antonio to take us for a ride and she also told me to call her Monique. She admired the little gold cross which my mother used to wear and on Monday she took me to a watchmaker who made three more holes in the strap of my watch so that it wouldn't dangle any more, and she bought for me a very thin thread made of silvery metal. The watchmaker joined the cross on to it and I was to wear it around my neck under my shirt. She said I had brown skin like a gipsy and soft like a girl's skin. She laughed when I blushed and told me that skin is called the same as the name of our town, only it is spelt differently.

On Friday we had a visitor: Marcel. He came at eleven which meant that he must have left very early and couldn't stop at the restaurant outside Orolon, where the owner made all those things out of piano wire. He brought me a note from Pedro in Spanish, and when I read it, I started to hiccup at once. Nothing more exciting had ever happened to me. It took my breath away. It said: "Dear Pablo, yesterday Manuel sent me a message to phone him and I went this morning to St. Etienne to give Marcel a letter for him. I might be coming to Pau to-morrow. The

important thing is that you should go as soon as you can to
see Manuel. He will ask you some questions. It is very
important and I want you to go at once. He lives at
45 Spanish Street, second floor, Manuel Artiguez. I am
coming to-morrow to Pau. Your friend, Pedro." There
was a postscript to it. " Don't tell a soul about this. It is
very secret and very important. Not even Marcel!"

I hated to lie to Monique but, of course, it was impossible not to. I said that I wanted to see posters of the
cinema and the funicular and she didn't much mind me
going. Neither did Marcel, though he was supposed to
have come to see *me* and not Monique. He brought a
bottle of wine for her as a present and they were talking
about the wine, which was white and had to be chilled a
little, and even in the ice-box it took at least half an hour
to cool.

" Come back in half an hour, it will be ready then," said
Monique. Marcel said something too and they argued
about it a little in French and then Monique translated:
" Marcel says it needs an hour, it is a sweet wine."

My hiccups lasted all the way to the Spanish Street.
My talent in geography came in very handy. I had been
only once to the Spanish Street before. Monique took me
to the Spanish grocer to buy the kind of Spanish sausages
which Antonio liked. She asked me to talk to the grocer
and while we were in the shop many people came in, all
Spanish, and they had a funny way of talking, mixing
French words with their Spanish, and the grocer said
" Merci " when he took their money.

When I got there I found the children playing football
in the Spanish Street. There were some girls among them,
kicking and screaming like the boys. But for these girls,

the street could have been in Pamplona, or any old Spanish
city. Of course, in Spain, the girls wouldn't play with the
boys and certainly not football which was a man's game.
The children were not allowed to kick the ball too high
on account of the washing hanging on lines stretching
beween the windows across the street. They played the
five-a-side game, one side consisting of six since the two
little ones counted only as one. They had a very soft ball,
the ginger-headed girl kicked it towards me and I caught
it in a manner that would have impressed even The Flute
who wasn't impressed by anything. The Flute thought he
could make a good goalkeeper out of me and he gave me
lessons on Sunday afternoons, but being such a bad shot,
he could never really test me. The ginger-haired girl and
a tall boy, called Julio, came running. In no time they
surrounded me, shouting, asking questions. They wanted
to know if I was Spanish, whether I could ride a bicycle,
and offered me a place in the team. At any other time I
would have felt honoured. I drank the sweet wine of
success, wanting more. Marcel's whole bottle of wine could
not have intoxicated me more.

"I can't," I said. "Not now. I'm on my way to see
Manuel Artiguez."

I looked around. Nobody had fainted. A small aggressive boy with a torn shirt took the ball from me.

"Let him wait."

"He won't run away," shouted another.

They were not at all impressed. Surely they did not
comprehend.

"I mean the famous Artiguez!"

Julio wondered: "What's he famous for?"

I gasped. Were they so stupid? So ignorant?

"He has killed more carabineros than any other man alive! Don't you know?"

The girl ran her ten fingers through her ginger hair in despair. "He has killed nothing but cockroaches for years."

"He hasn't crossed the border for years, he doesn't dare," declared the aggressive boy. He unlaced the rubber vent of the ball in an effort to blow it up. I felt choking. To add to my misery, I started hiccuping again. I knew from experience that no argument brought forward between hiccups sounded convincing.

"In . . . in . . . in Spain . . . in Spain there's a . . . price of a hun-hun . . . hundred thousand pe-pesetas on his h-h-head," I stammered.

"That makes three hundred thousand," mocked Julio, and all screamed with laughter. " I don't believe it."

"I s . . . s . . . saw it with my own eyes," I argued. "On a p-poster outside the policia in Pam . . . Pam . . . Pamplona. I swear!"

The boy blowing up the ball began to lace it up again. "Oh, let him go. He's a mouse, too."

I drew myself up and balled my fist: "Who's a mouse?"

He got frightened and backed away. "HE!"

"HE who?" I wanted to know.

Julio was not afraid. "Your Manuel! And if you say no, you're a mouse, too." He snatched the ball from the other boy and kicked it into the gutter. They swept after it like a whirlwind. For a second I felt like flying after them and murdering the lot. Then I remembered what my father used to tell me: "Take a deep breath, Pablo." I took one and then another very deep one. I crossed the street, walking towards number 45. The girl kicked the ball deliberately at me. I ducked and did not touch it.

The moment I passed them, a squeaky voice called after me: "Mighty mouse's got a visitor: the little mouse!" I turned as quick as lightning but could not discover whose voice it was. I went into number 45 and started to climb the rickety stairs.

2

MIGUEL. MIGUEL-SOMETHING. His other name begins with an R. Rodriguez? No, that wasn't it. Ramones? No. Moreno! That's it, Miguel Moreno. It didn't begin with an R after all. But there is an important R in Moreno. Anyway, he was quite a fellow. A good fighter. The civil war wasn't lost because of him, or because of any of the old types. He saved my life in the battle of Currentes and I saved his when he got wounded in the fields of Cero. I found him lying in the tall corn. Poor corn it was, full of red poppies, in some spots there were more poppies than corn. He groaned, stretched out on a bed of corn and red poppies, but when I looked closer, I saw that not all the red was poppies, but specks of his blood. Now, what makes me think of Miguel Moreno? He was about fifty-five and he always wanted to show off his strength and stamina. When we blocked a road, he carried heavier logs than any of us, staggering under the weight, moaning

33   B

and sweating, but grinning. The general gave him easier assignments, but he wouldn't hear of it. When we crossed the Pallaresa that frozen February, he was first to dive into the icy river, his teeth chattering like faraway machine-guns. If a scout was wanted, he jumped to volunteer. He used to return exhausted, sick with fear. We couldn't understand what made him do it. Then the day when I looked up his wife in Huesca, a little old, dried-up woman, to give her what remained of her husband after the siege of the village of Mesta, she put me into the picture.

" He was ashamed of his years. He always wanted to prove he wasn't old."

I couldn't quite believe it. But I do now. I lie on this bed when I'm on my own, drifting between sleep and wakefulness. Even to stagger to the bath is an effort. But if people are around, I move swiftly. I never use my reading glasses when young men are looking, I try to make out the headlines with smarting eyes.

Fifty-six is not really old. Not nowadays. Didn't I raid Pamplona nineteen months ago? Viñolas and his guardia civil! I made them look stupid. I shall make them look even more stupid the next time. My eyes are improving. My memory is improving. Didn't I find the name of Miguel Moreno just now? I remembered the name of Pedro's village this morning when I phoned him. I seemed to remember everything. Let me see: Pilar's hospital in Pamplona is called Santa Cruz, the street: Calle de la Cruz. My hearing has never been better. I could hear someone coming up the stairs right now. Show me the young man who could hear it from this bed. Light steps passing my door. Now they have stopped.

I jumped from bed. Was it the old woman from the third floor taking a breather? If it was, I would hear her blowing. There was not a sound. The floorboards creaked outside. Then came the shy, hesitating knock. Come in! A little boy of ten or eleven opened the door. They used to come, the small boys, in the old days, they used to follow me all over the streets, I was a sort of a hero to them. Now they followed everyone, pulling faces behind your back and if you turned, they looked as innocent as an unborn babe.

The boy stood in the door, staring as if he had seen a ghost.

"Where do I find Mr. Artiguez?" he asked. When I told him that I was Artiguez, he seemed doubtful. "*Manuel* Artiguez?" He must have seen a picture of me when I was young, for he just stared. He stared at my head and my neck, both of which were a little stiff since two bullets had been removed, just about nineteen months ago.

"Come in, or get out!"

He came in, closed the door, and resumed staring. I asked who he was and what he wanted? It transpired he knew Pedro, got a note from him to come to see me. I was supposed to ask some questions of him. It sounded curious for I had spoken to Pedro only a few hours ago, and for the life of me I couldn't recollect wanting to ask anything of anybody.

I washed my face, buttoned up my shirt and decided to get rid of him.

"Now run along, boy, what's-your-name."

He suddenly lost his shyness and turned quite impertinent. "I've already given you my name."

I told him not to be insolent and if he had mentioned his name before, to do so a second time. Pablo Dages was his name, the son of José Dages. Of course I remem-

bered José Dages. Carlos brought me the news about him
some four weeks ago.

"Who's Carlos?" the boy asked. I told him that
Carlos was a friend who went to Pamplona every now and
then, taking things and bringing things.

"Smuggler?" he inquired.

"What I said doesn't make him a smuggler yet. Tell
me about your father. Did they beat him at the policia?"

He remained silent.

"How long did they keep him there?"

"Four days."

"And after four days he died?"

He shook his head. "After four days they took him
to the hospital. He lived another nine days."

"Did they let you see him?" I asked, just to say something.

"They did. During the day. At night they chased me
away. But in the day-time they let me into the ward at
the hospital."

Pilar had been taken to hospital in Pamplona. That was
it. Of course, Pedro had mentioned the boy, but that
cursed line was so full of noises I could not hear half of
what he said. Pilar was sick and wanted to see me, so
I would have to go to Pamplona. It would be tricky to get
into that hospital, even by night. In any case I ought to
know the layout of the place. Carlos had brought over a
photograph of the street. It was a poor picture, you could
see only the corner of Calle de la Cruz and the square.
Now this boy, here, who had been in the hospital many
times might help me. There was nothing wrong with my
memory, I just couldn't hear what Pedro said owing to
that clatter on the line.

Of course I had to be careful. You never knew where

you were with boys. Their fancy took the strangest turns. They loved railway engines, but would stand along the line and throw stones at them. Someone scribbled something on my door a week ago, I bet it was one of those little scoundrels. They had it from their elders though. I knew what they were saying in the bistros, in the backyards, and at home. In their view, a man had to prove himself all the time. Haven't I crossed into Spain more often than any man alive? Three and four times every year ever since '39. Was there anybody with a greater price on his head? What the bloody hell have they got out of me risking my life? They loved to read about it in their papers in the morning. Sitting on their arses at the breakfast table. They wouldn't understand that a man got tired of doing the same thing year after year. What is there left to do over there? I have raided the banks, I have burned the post office, I have done every blasphemy to the priests and desecrated churches. What more did they want from me? They said I was getting old. They did not say it, really, they whispered it. Carlos told me only the other day, they talked about my losing my nerve. I, *losing* my nerve! I could hold a spoon with outstretched arm without a flicker of shaking. I slept as soundly as a baby-angel. If anything, it was that I slept *too* much. Why shouldn't I? There was nothing to do here, I had got enough money tucked away for as long as I lived, I had been a good fighter during the war, and I had gone on fighting for another twenty years. That should be enough for anyone: it was enough for me. I was not afraid of anybody or anything. But I was getting cautious. I admit that I was getting cautious. That was a virtue, not a sin. If Pilar got worse, I'd go to Pamplona. Not otherwise. They could chalk on my door what they bloody well liked. It wouldn't sway me this way or that. And if I caught one of those little brutes poking fun at me, I would smack his filthy bottom and if his father objected I would bang his head on the wall until he made his brute learn a lesson. And if this boy, here, thought that he'd go downstairs to tell funny stories about Manuel Artiguez he, too, would get what was coming to him.

I went to the window to see if there were any little brutes waiting downstairs. There were none.

" How's your memory?" I asked Pablo Dages.

" Not too bad."

" What's the name of the street of the hospital?"

" Calle de la Cruz."

" What's the building at the corner, coming from the square?"

" Right or left?"

" Left."

" The bank. It's got a clock over the entrance and an iron grille when it's shut for the night. A man opens the grille at nine o'clock. He wears uniform. He has a gun in his pocket. In the hip pocket. Are you going to rob the bank?"

I had got the photograph Carlos brought over and glossed over his question. " How do you know he has got a gun?"

" I saw it with my own eyes. When he pushes up the grille to reach the catch, his coat slips right up, you can see the handle of his gun."

He had quite a memory, this boy. He could describe the entrance, the hall, the staircase, the men's ward of the hospital. Of course he had never entered the women's ward but that was probably identical. The only difference being that one was situated to the left, the other to the right, as seen from the main staircase.

"Are you going to raid the hospital?" he asked. He got quite excited about it. His eyes were shining, suddenly he shed all his shyness, he was a different boy. I told him that I had no intention of carrying out a raid. Who had ever heard of raiding a hospital? But—I *had* to get into that hospital somehow.

Pablo Dages knew quite a lot about me. He had seen the poster showing my face outside the guardia civil in Pamplona. A lousy photograph, no one would recognise you from that, he said. He knew about Pilar, too. He had seen her often, going about, leaning on her crooked walking-stick, shopping for food, people pointing at her: there goes Manuel Artiguez's mother. Sometimes Pablo strolled in front of the house she lived in and when she happened to look out of the window, he would ask her if there was anything she wanted, anything he could do for her. But she had never accepted help from Pablo, or indeed from anybody else. A proud woman, a hard old stick, that was Pilar. I told Pablo that she had got very sick lately, only a few days ago they had taken her to the hospital of Santa Cruz. Carlos had visited her there. She got mellower as old people sometimes do. She had only one wish: to see her son. So that's why I had to go. If she didn't get any better, that is. Carlos was due back to-morrow, or on Sunday at the latest. Pablo didn't seem to take it in.

"When is it going to be?" he asked.

"It depends."

"To-night?"

"Not to-night."

"To-morrow?"

"If I have to."

" I hope you have to," he said and I told him what I thought of his attitude, for he knew well by now that I would go, but only if Pilar got worse. He considered this. " You haven't been across lately. . . ."

" I have."

" When?"

" Nineteen months ago."

" That's not lately."

Now, this sounded just like all that bloody gossip in the bistros. I was sure that someone had been talking about me in front of him. I got hold of him and he really got the wind up. He admitted that the children *had* been talking, but he, Pablo, didn't believe a word. *What* they were saying, he wouldn't divulge. I let him go. He was an honest boy, eager to help me. And what a memory he had!

I sent him home for lunch, warning him not to tell a soul what he had heard from me. I watched him going from the window, saw him avoiding some children who crossed his path. I couldn't hear what they were saying, but I saw the grin on Pablo's face, a rather superior sort of grin.

Nothing was wrong with my eyesight. True, I needed those glasses to read the papers, or for this photograph of Calle de la Cruz, but if a man could see the grin on a boy's face from this height, he had nothing to worry about his eyesight. I sat on the bed thinking. Perhaps this was my lucky day. Finding this boy seemed a bit of blue sky in the general gloom. If I had to go over, I needed precise knowledge of every detail. I'd take Pedro with me and perhaps another. I hoped Pedro would come with me. He didn't say no on the telephone, but he might not have heard properly what I was saying because of the awful noise on the line. On the other hand, he had sent me this boy to give me the information about the hospital. This meant that he did understand about the necessity of my going. Necessity is not what I mean. It depends on the news Carlos brings. I hope for Pilar's sake, she is better. And also for Pedro's sake.

The girl, Teresa, came to clean the flat. I knew that she had an affair with Carlos, I heard them often enough playing about in the other room where Carlos slept when he happened to be in Pau. She was convinced that Carlos would marry her, but I knew that scores of girls thought that Carlos would marry them. I called her over to the bed, but she refused to come. I told her that I could have any woman I fancied, if I wanted to. She laughed and said:

"If! If I had a moustache and a few other things, I would be a man."

I slapped her bottom and she ran out without finishing her cleaning.

I lay down on the bed. I could do the thinking I had to do better lying down. Now, let's see what are the alternatives? Carlos went yesterday, the chances were he wouldn't be back before to-morrow night, or, most likely, on Sunday. Alternative number one: Pilar is better. Then I don't have to go at all. Next time I'll send her some money again and a warm coat for the winter. She will scold me for the coat, she will call me a fool, sending her a coat for the winter in June. But she will be pleased all the same, thinking of her son being sure that she wouldn't die in the summer. Now, number two: Pilar is worse. Then I'll have to dig up my gun and perhaps Pedro's gun, we might take some hand-grenades too. We'll have to test the guns in the forest and we'll have to test the hand-

grenades. I'm against making a show of it. When one's
visiting one's sick mother, it's not the time to fool about
raiding the guardia or anything else. Of course, if I'm
forced to use my gun, I'll use it. But no fooling around
this time. Just coming swiftly and before it gets around,
we'll be gone. We might raid a frontier post though, so
that the papers have something to write about. " It is
believed that Manuel Artiguez has paid another of his
famous visits to Spain. French police investigated but, as
always, he had a perfect alibi." I could leave the matter of
an alibi to Carlos. He is a perfect wizard at arranging
alibis. Right. Going Sunday evening, back Monday.
I might go with Pedro to the bistros on Monday. We'll
listen to all those monkeys talking about us. Pretending
that we can't hear them talking. And this time, I'll do
something about moving from Pau to another place.
Somewhere where people don't expect you to show your
courage all the time, where you can just live. A cottage,
a few acres of land, I would like to grow my own vine.
There is something about inviting your friend to your own
cellar and telling him: " Take the light, Pedro, go down
the steps and bring up another bottle." Why, for heaven's
sake, haven't I done it a long time ago? I've got the money.
I've risked my life many times for that money, it's high
time that I had some good from it. I would like to have
fruit trees in my vineyard, peaches and cherries and a
walnut tree in front of the cottage for shade and smell.
And for the oil. Nothing better than walnut-oil for salads,
for cooking, even for oiling a gun. I mean a shotgun for
hunting the deer. I would never have believed that there
were so many deer in these parts. They say all sorts of
foreigners come here every year to hunt. I've seen fine
deer on occasions, when I used to come back from a raid

in Spain, just before sunrise, they feed on the edge of the forest, herds of a dozen or more. You pick out one, fire your rifle, you watch the deer drop and the herd goes on grazing as if nothing had happened. Perhaps I will ask Pedro about a cottage. He might know of one going, one close to his own place. It would be fun to be a neighbour of old Pedro. We stood side by side when we got our money, why shouldn't we convert it into properties lying side by side?

Pablo was late. He arrived after three and mumbled something about his French aunt having been late with lunch. He had some wine, not much, he said, for he wanted to be quite sober while giving me the layout about the hospital. Shortly afterwards the postman brought a letter from Pilar, written in her ancient scribble, telling me that she had been taken to hospital, where she got good care and everything she wanted. Her letter cheered me up no end. But Pablo seemed to have taken into his silly head that it was better for me to go. Even if Pilar's health improved. I told him that he was a fool. Certainly getting a letter from her meant that she had not been watched in the hospital. Not by the police anyway. If she ever wrote from home, the letter took a week, a sure sign that Viñolas's men had intercepted and opened it. Usually, I could see the marks of violence on it, the fine cut of the razor into the envelope, where the patience of the pirates had snapped while applying the hot knife to the seal. There was no reference in the letter about Pilar wishing to see me. That, of course, meant nothing. She would never risk writing such things to me. She addressed the letter, as she always did, to Madame Berthelot, the woman who owned this place and from whom I had rented it for the past three years.

" All right, boy, let's get on with our business. Now, then. What comes next to the bank? The hospital? Right." I drew two parallel lines signifying the street. Pablo paused after each question, deliberating in silence. Through his downcast eyes you could peer into the workshop of his brain, all the wheels turning, cogwheels, fly-wheels, axles, spindles, spools and shafts.

" Next to the hospital is a laundry. A big laundry. It has seven delivery vans, I counted them. The vans drive in from another street parallel to the Calle de la Cruz. They drive out here, though. Sort of one-way traffic."

" Good. It means that there are some buildings which have two entrances from two different streets."

" Yes. The hospital has two entrances. All the ambulances arrive on the other side. They brought my father in from the other side."

" Right. Now, do you remember if the roofs of the buildings are joined together, or is there a gap between them?"

" They are joined together."

" Are you sure?"

" I saw a chimney-sweep walking from one roof to another. All roofs are joined together in the street. I mean all roofs on one side."

" Now, let's get back to the hospital. Is there any street-lighting in front of it?"

" Plenty."

" Is there a strong light in the hall?"

" Yes. But after ten o'clock, half the light is turned off by the night porter."

" When does the night porter take over?"

" At nine. He's a little man. You'll have no difficulty with him."

" Where is his place? Where does he stay when on duty?"

" He has a little lodge. Sort of cabin. There are two doors to it, one leads to the hall, the other into the store room."

" What do they store in the store room?"

" Everything. Beds, screens, chamber-pots, instruments. It has another door from the corridor. There's a store-keeper in the store room. Sometimes he goes in from the porter's lodge. But the people who come to fetch things go in from the corridor."

" Now, the stairs. Are they wide stairs?"

" Wide up to the first floor. From there on there are two narrow stairs."

" Which side is the women's ward?"

" Left. The men's ward is on the right."

I tried to memorise it, repeating several times: women's ward left, men's ward right.

" Are there many people on the stairs at night-time?"

" Not many. Doctors mostly. And nurses."

We went on a long time, I asking, he answering. I made notes, he watched me like an apprentice watches his master. Suddenly he plucked up courage and asked me if I were going to get even with Viñolas? I told him that I was not, not this time.

" But—if you happened to bump into him?" he asked hopefully.

" I'll try not to bump into anybody."

He was most useful and rather touching in his eager-ness. When I asked him what I could get for him as a present, he shook his head. I urged him not to be shy about it.

He said: "There is one thing. . . ."

I tried to encourage him. He hesitated. Then, at long last, he came out with it.

"Try to bump into Viñolas."

PAMPLONA is a fine city at any time, but never finer than in June. The best time of a June day is the early morning and nobody has yet invented a better way to start the day than riding in the park. I liked this horse. What could be going on in the mind of such a horse? Yesterday, my pet, and all your days before, you lived in the country, your rider had been a lightweight fellow, a little man, who stood over you when you were born, who patted and stroked you daily, who trained you and rode you. Now you are in the city, nervous and suspicious, carrying a master twice as heavy. Don't fret, my love, I'll be a good master to you. Perhaps you have brought me luck, my lamb. If this seems a red-letter day to you, it might be a far greater day for your new master. You have certainly brought luck to your former owner. He would have been investigated for his political activities but for you, my little one. You might bring *me* luck, since this might turn out to be the most important day of my life. So, hold up your head, my

47

jewel, step high and proudly, you are carrying the chief of police on your back.

Sorry that I had to change your name, old girl, but Rosana is a name taboo in my family. You will be called Teresa from now, a nice solid name, the same as my wife's. She is a nice solid, fine lady, and she will adore you for your name. She will bring you so much hard sugar that the vet will have to look after your teeth, she will ride you once or twice a month, always after sunset, and you'll find her a mere feather after carrying me. And she is getting lighter every week and her skin getting too large for her flesh and no doctor and no praying seems to help her. I went with her to church last night and prayed with her, kneeling in the cool darkness of the cathedral while the procession of choir boys in white and the priests leading them, marched round and round. I loved the coolness, the stained-glass windows, the singing in harmony, the clearness of the boys' sopranos, the deep chords of the priests, but when Teresa whispered into my ear to pray for her, I cheated her and prayed for myself. And I thought how difficult it must be for the Lord to sort out the wishes worthy to be granted from those of no merit. Manuel Artiguez might be praying at this very moment for success. Compared with my bad fortune in fighting him, he had the edge on me all these years. How was this possible? What made his prayers more acceptable than my own? I was a sinner, I couldn't deny it. I had a mistress, but I did not love her, it was nothing but a carnal relationship. I gave her what she needed and I got what I could not do without. I had never been unfaithful to Teresa while she had her looks. Was it my fault that she had lost all her attraction for me, or for anybody else for that matter? Every healthy man needs a woman from time to time.

Was it worse to have one mistress instead of many? A man in my position must be careful about his affairs. I visited Rosana in the lunch-hour every weekday, but never on Saturdays and never on Sundays. To have an affair in the day-time was not a serious affair, everybody would agree with that. I never spoke to my mistress about my home life, I never mentioned the name of my wife, as so many do. I even told her that I loved my wife, that my family was for me holy and she understood. When I heard from her that she had a source of nylon stockings, making a few pesetas on selling them, I bought six pairs for Teresa and both women loved me for it, but I had pangs of conscience for many days. Later, I bought more stockings for my daughter, Julita. That couldn't have been notched against me in heaven either, since it gave pleasure to three people and did not harm anybody. Against my trivial sins, stood the bandit's infamy, brutality, his deadly sins. Still, in our encounters up to now, I was the loser every time. Oh, well, perhaps this is how things had to be. Every success is regarded higher when it comes after continuous failure. Every victory sweeter when it was hard earned.

It will be fifteen years come August when I came to head the guardia civil in Pamplona. There will be no cele-brations if Artiguez is still at large. I'll get a kiss from Teresa in the morning, another from Rosana during lunch, and I'll get an inkwell from the officers on my staff. I know it, for Lieutenant Zapater asked me only the other day, why I kept that old glass one on my desk? I'll get a letter from the Ministry in Madrid, signed by the permanent secretary, wishing me every success in the future. I have been wondering why they hadn't replaced me a long time ago. Now I knew. No one wanted to come here to take the job. When they transferred me from Huesca, I was credited with

trapping Ramon Morales. They thought I'd get Manuel
Artiguez, too. Holy Mother, was that fifteen years ago?
They had expected me to catch him in a year. When the
bandit started to roam farther afield, when he raided the
bank in Barcelona, when he robbed that train near Irun,
they said: Let Viñolas organise his forces, give him time,
Rome wasn't built in a day. I tried my best. I fought
him, I went after him, I collected money to pay informers,
but he slipped out of my traps each time. Still, they can't
say that I had achieved nothing. After all, Artiguez has
not been seen in Spain for nineteen months and seven days.

Several church clocks were striking eight o'clock. I
turned the horse towards the sandy path leading to the road.
Don't be afraid, my little beauty, this bus will be stopped
by the traffic policeman to let us pass, he knows who we
are. Where would that bandit be at this very moment?
Has he started already? Was he hiding somewhere on the
French side of the mountain waiting for darkness to fall,
or has he got the audacity to come in daylight? When
was he going to cross? The frontier patrols were doubled
at every likely place. He might be caught by one of them.
He might be shot in the mountains and I shall be sick with
sterile, wretched frustration, though *I* laid the trap and *I*
organised the hunt. No, to make it a true triumph, he
should be conquered here, in Pamplona. Somewhere on
the approaches to the hospital. I have deserved that, after
fifteen years, I have deserved that. I'll buy a thousand
candles for the cathedral. I'll go to Lourdes and I'll take
Rosana also, to fulfil her dearest wish to do a pilgrimage to
Lourdes. Forgive me, Oh Lord, I didn't mean that seriously. I would take Teresa, my wife, with me. So that
she could bathe in the holy pool and could be cured and
put on weight again. I vow to do that. I promise to

forgo the bullfights this season and next, and you know how much I love the bullfights. And I pledge, if it has to be, that I shall never see Rosana again. I undertake this in good faith. Just let me rid us all from this curse, from this blasphemous beast.

At the police stables, I told the duty sergeant that I wouldn't be riding the gelding in the future, it could go back on general duty as I had bought this mare and I wanted it to be looked after properly and to be given the same rations as the gelding. They all came to admire her, down to the last stable boy and she got a foretaste of what it meant to be Miguel Viñolas's horse. Paco, my driver, was waiting. He had no message for me, though he came from the policia and had asked for messages, guessing that I should want to know. He said that Lieutenant Zapater had already arrived in his office. What, in heaven's name, was he doing there at seven-thirty? The man had been a nuisance ever since he joined the force. I would have got rid of him long ago, but he had an uncle in the Ministry, in Madrid, one of those nasty types who, at the District Commissioners' Convention, asked me bombastic questions in connection with our record of crime in Pamplona, during the last five years, singling me out in particular and making me the laughing stock of the assembly. Of course, as everybody knew, the record of the Pamplona police during the past couple of years had been one of the best in the whole country. Before that we had a thin time due to Artiguez, but why bring it up when all those present knew it, if not to underline it before the whole conference?

The car stopped in front of the policia. Outside the entrance, on the bill-board, I saw the large poster showing the picture of Artiguez, offering 100,000 pesetas for anyone who would lead the police to his capture, dead or alive.

The price on his head had been raised to a hundred thousand after his raid on the church, but nobody had collected the money, nobody had even tried to collect it. It might be collected to-night.

As soon as I got into my office, Zapater came to see me. He reported:

"I checked some of the likely frontier-posts, nothing unusual."

"What do you expect, man?"

He grinned and explained that he meant The Smuggler, not Artiguez. This, also, was too silly for words. He knew as well as I did that The Smuggler crossed the border always at one particular point, which we had agreed, so there was no earthly reason to check other places. Of course The Smuggler should have already been across the border if he kept to our prearranged time-table, but The Smuggler never did, you had to give him some latitude. Being a police-informer, he had to be careful. He was moving among men who were fast with their knives and their guns. A hundred thousand pesetas meant a fortune to most people, but I, for one, held that if The Smuggler kept his part of the bargain, he had earned every one of those hundred thousand pesetas. Zapater seemed to think the same.

"If we get him to-night," Zapater said, "what are we going to do about all that money?"

This fellow got on my nerves.

"What do you mean IF?"

"Well, something might go wrong. It has done in the past."

"This is not the past. In the past we never had any luck. This time we have. In the past we had to spread our forces. This time we know where to expect him and we have done everything."

He nodded.

" I called at the hospital on the way to the office——"

I got furious. Is he trying to sabotage the whole thing? Why go to the hospital? Do we know whom we can trust in the hospital? Eighty-six people work there, one of them could be a sympathiser, one of them probably is. Hadn't we agreed that we let the hospital alone till this afternoon? We move in after lunch and not before, and when we do, we seal the place. Artiguez is due to come over to-night. We planned it with The Smuggler and we agreed, all of us, to keep it secret till the very last minute.

" No one saw me, I went straight to the matron's office."

" No one saw you? What about the doorman? What about the secretary?"

" But the doorman and the secretary are trustworthy. Both falangists."

" I don't trust anybody!"

I stopped in time. I almost said I didn't trust even a falangist. I wondered if he guessed. I was anything but sure about Zapater. The Ministry in Madrid seemed to be too well-informed about local matters. Where did they get their information? From people like Zapater? Probably every district of the guardia civil had its Zapater. I hastened to add:

" I trust you and a few like you, that's all. In our game, the fewer people who know the better."

He agreed. He spoke to the matron and she had told him that Pilar had had an uncomfortable night.

" But the matron said Pilar is made of steel."

" Is she taking food?"

" Not since the day before yesterday."

" Does she talk?"

" She hadn't uttered a word ever since she'd been brought in."

" For heaven's sake, Zapater, don't utter a word either."

" No, sir."

" You know that I haven't told it even to my wife?"

I could read his thoughts. He said to himself: I wonder if he has told it to his mistress? Well, I hadn't. I regarded my private life as a closed book. Or as *two* closed books, anyway.

We discussed the proceedings. As soon as The Smuggler arrived, we'd hold a conference. He should be brought here in a closed car and kept here. I had the money in my desk, the whole hundred thousand, in five envelopes. I had been careful to draw it from the bank in five instalments as a precaution. The bank might have a clerk, a sympathiser, who could put two and two together. I wanted to have the money ready for The Smuggler the moment he was entitled to it. The news among informers travels faster than anywhere else. I wanted them to know that I paid promptly and without fail. As soon as we heard what The Smuggler had to report, I'd give the signal for my forces to move in. We had had them standing by since last night, the army platoon with two armoured cars, the toughest men of our own guardia, two machine-guns in the laundry window, submachine-guns for selected men, the whole operation had been mapped out to the smallest detail, except that no time for it had been fixed. Nothing would be done, not a word revealed, till mid-afternoon. Except, of course, in case The Smuggler brought the unlikely news that Artiguez was risking to come in broad daylight.

" Ring up the sergeant in Elizondo, Zapater. Check

about the safe conduct for The Smuggler. There are bound to be some new men on the job since we've doubled the patrols. I want him here as soon as possible. And check whether a car is waiting to get him here."

He went and I took out the plan of operation. I called in Sanchez and he reported on the arrangements for my temporary office.

"I've chosen the flat here." He pointed out the house

opposite the hospital on the plan. "It belongs to a woman on the third floor. We brought her in this morning."

I asked him what story he had told her.

"I said that we expected a raid on the laundry, as you said, sir."

"Was she difficult?"

"Not at all, sir. And she doesn't mind being here for a day or two. I promised her a telephone."

This sounded very strange. "Why a telephone?"

"She's a hussy, sir. Sort of call-girl. Needs a phone for business and she's been trying to get one for a long time. They're installing it now."

"Fast work, Sanchez."

"I thought we'd need a phone there to-night."

Now here was an efficient policeman. And one who knew his place. He reported that a walkie-talkie had been tried out between the flat and the laundry and proved to be working satisfactorily. It would serve us well to communicate with the hospital and the other units spread around it. Zapater came back. Elizondo had no news of The Smuggler yet. It worried me a little. I figured he should be over the border by now. If he crossed before sunrise, he should have contacted one of our patrols. I hoped nothing had gone wrong. O, my Lord, don't let me down this time. In addition to that pilgrimage to Lourdes and taking my wife instead of Rosana, I vow to give away my new horse. I'll give it back to its owner, if you think I shouldn't have taken it from him. And, perhaps, Lourdes is too easy for a pilgrimage, just across the border. I undertake to go all the way to Rome and with my *wife* and I shall never see Rosana again. I'll see her just once more to-day since she is expecting me. I shall have to prepare her for

the break, otherwise she will fly off the handle and make
a scandal.

" I want to see that woman, that call-girl," I said, and
as soon as I had said it, I was sorry. Now I'm making
promises and vows and what do I do? I have no business
to see that woman. On the other hand, I'm not breaking
any vows by seeing her. It is indeed my duty to talk to
her. I'm not interested in her looks, but I must know
whether we are to expect people to come to see her so that
we can deal with eventualities. We might have to put up a
sign downstairs on the door that she has gone away. Or we
might have to post a plainclothes man to deal with visitors.
Or, better, if she is expecting people, we ought to send
them a message to stop them.

Sanchez brought her and left us alone. She was very
pretty and very young, not more than twenty-two, if that
much. She came from Huesca and I told her that I knew
Huesca well, my station prior to Pamplona was there.
She seemed a little frightened at first, but women regain
their poise very fast. That is if you give them a chance.
She had strong white teeth and when she flashed her eyes
they fired like a twin-barrelled gun. With a little help,
shoes, a shade longer skirt and tighter, of course, she could
look absolutely stunning. She had no steady boy-friend;
if someone wished to see her, he had to telephone a woman
on the first floor, a friend much older than she was. That
was easy. She seemed quite happy about the room Sanchez
had given her for the day and I promised to find out later
if she had everything she wanted.

At eleven a.m. I phoned Elizondo myself. Still no trace
of The Smuggler. I told the sergeant to send a man up
the mountain to make sure that no patrol had seen him.
I told him to get through the second they had located him.

The sergeant asked if a man whom they had caught during the night, near the Verderiz, and who had been sent to Pamplona under escort, had arrived. The fellow was Luis Dages, cousin of that fool, José Dages, who had been so stubborn a few weeks ago and who died consequently of some old liver ailment. The prisoner did arrive and was waiting to be brought before me. I had known him for years, a small-time thug, who did a little poaching, a little smuggling, frightened, determined not to get into trouble for his old age, but too poor to live an honest life. At one time I thought he would make an informer, but since José Dages died, Luis was no good to me, his only important contacts being through his cousin. They caught him in the forest, this side of the border, so I knew exactly what he would say: he went fishing, fishing without a licence being the smallest offence. Whenever a smuggler was caught, he always tried to prove that he went fishing. Most of them bought a trout from a licensed fisherman before they set out for France and carried the burden of a complete tackle, just for proof of being anglers. We knew it and they knew that we knew. I had no time to waste with The Flute, as they called him. He grinned shyly.

" I just wanted to catch something for Sunday, sir."

" Bad luck, Flute. Instead, they've caught you. Have you been in France lately?"

His face showed consternation.

" Why would I go to France, sir?"

" To visit friends. To bring a few watches to Pamplona."

" Watches, sir? I don't need any watch. I can tell the time from the position of the sun."

He looked dried-up, sunburnt, his skin, in want of a shave, had the semblance of a cornfield after gathering in the harvest. He must have guessed my thought.

" I'm an old man, sir. Waiting to die."

He said it simply and suddenly I felt sorry for him. I nodded to the sergeant, he understood. It meant that The Flute could go. I called the old fellow back from the door.

" And if you hear of someone crossing the border, let me know. One hundred pesetas and free traffic for you."

" Thank you, sir. But they never tell me."

I thought I discerned the wisp of a grin on his face. Pity to let him go so cheaply. These people know no gratitude. He'll probably tell to-night a tall story of how he outwitted Viñolas himself. Let him tell his story. There might be no listeners for it to-night. They'll be telling another story. Christ in heaven, I don't wish to exaggerate, but I did act kindly and mercifully towards The Flute. Please make a note of it. I shall always be kind and I shall go to Rome with my wife and won't go to the bullfights for two years and I shall give back that horse to its owner and finish with Rosana and I'll buy for that poor call-girl another skirt, a few pairs of stockings and a pair of nice shoes. No, sorry, I didn't mean that. Just to prove how seriously I mean it, I'll go now to Rosana and after lunch I'll say whatever is necessary to start ending our affair. I'll give her ten thousand pesetas so that she will keep her mouth shut. I'll get the money somehow, I might sell the mare, Teresa, she is worth more than that and the horse-dealer would give me twice what she is worth. He's always in trouble and wants to be on good terms with the guardia civil. Of course I'll need the money from selling the mare for the trip to Rome. . . . If I finish Manuel Artiguez to-night, I can do anything, I don't have to sell the mare at all, it'll be easy to get the money. The mare should go back to where she came from.

At half past one, there was still no news of The Smuggler.

We checked and rechecked with Elizondo and they had done the same with all the patrols. This meant that he did not cross during the night and that again meant that something had not gone according to plan. Now, let's think it out logically. The Smuggler had played a double game and warned Artiguez. But why should he do that? That bandit wouldn't give him a hundred thousand pesetas and nothing but money mattered to The Smuggler. Or, someone had given The Smuggler away. But who knew about him? To the frontier-guards, he was just a smuggler who, when caught, had to be taken at once to Pamplona for questioning. Only the sergeant, in Elizondo, knew that The Smuggler was more than that, for he had to provide transport for him when he asked for it. But even the sergeant did not know the connection between The Smuggler and Artiguez. He had never been to my office, I was careful to see him at my home only. There was another variation. What if The Smuggler had to cross with Manuel himself? In that case, they would be lying low together till nightfall. Or The Smuggler might have been taken ill, suddenly, and the bandit would turn up to-night. I had to take the risk, we had to move in by four p.m. I had chosen four o'clock since visiting time in the hospital ended then and I wanted everything to be normal up to the very last minute. I told Zapater that I was going out for lunch, but I wished to hear any news on The Smuggler as soon as it came in. I watched his face for any sign of impertinence but couldn't discover any. Of course, it would be just like him to think: even on a day like this he goes to visit his mistress.

Paco sweated as he drove me through the steaming furnace of the city, almost deserted. How calm, how ordinary everything was. The streets, the drive, the heat,

the cafés, the open door of the passage, unlocked by the
caretaker, waiting for my car to enter so that I could get
out without being spotted from the street, the blue light
filtering through the coloured panes of the portal frame,
the coolness of the stairs and the magic of the door being
flung open at the creaking of the boards on the landing and
Rosana standing hidden behind the door, all these were as
on any ordinary day. I kissed her cheek, complimented her
on her new hair-do, inhaled her scent and the freshness of
her skin while she brought me up to date on what had
happened to her since yesterday. She asked my help in
getting some tickets for the opening day of the bullfights
for a relative, while the maid served lunch in the dark
dining-room, with the shutters closed against the sun. She
asked about the new horse and about the office.

" You look worried. Is it Zapater again?"

I told her it wasn't Zapater and I had no worries except
the usual ones. She asked if *she* was a worry to me and
if so, did I include her among the usual ones? She had
a sort of nonsensical way of talking, I liked it as a change
after the office and I liked her long legs as they caught the
eye when she walked, though she held her dressing-gown
with both hands. Some women have legs good for nothing
but conveying their owners from place to place. Others
have legs to be admired. Some legs are working legs,
others are lazy legs. I had decided to delay telling her
about not going to Lourdes this year. I thought Lourdes
was a holy place, a place of pilgrimage, why should it be
pleasing to the Lord to refuse to take somebody who was
so anxious to go? She had been planning this trip ever
since she had mentioned it for the first time just before
Christmas. Out of the blue one day, she said: " You can
go by car via Dancharinea and I'll take the train and we'll

meet in Bayonne." And a few days later: " Can we stop
in Pau? Pau has the best shops, I want to gloat over the
shop windows for an hour while you take your apéritif.
I know Pau as well as Pamplona. My husband used to take
me there."

I had, as always, my siesta after lunch, lying on the wide
sofa with the brown and white rug on it to save the plush
cover. She sat on the edge, holding her cool hand against
my forehead, worrying why I would not fall asleep. Once
the telephone rang but it was for the old lady on the ground
floor. Rosana took a message for her and reminded me that
I had promised to help the old lady to get her own line.
I made a note and remembered the girl who had got her
telephone with the help of the police this morning, and
made a comparison between her and Rosana. I wondered
if she had a cool hand. Then the church clock struck one
and it meant a quarter past three and I had to go. I asked
Rosana to pray for me to-night. She wanted to know why.
I answered: " It has something to do with Pau." She
put her arms around me gratefully and lovingly and I
wondered if I committed a sin by letting her think that
I meant the same thing she did.

There was still no news about The Smuggler. At four
o'clock, I spoke to the sergeant in Elizondo. He had been
on his motor-bike to the pass during the lunch-hour to
check for himself. He found that one of the patrol huts
had been cut off by a freak thunderstorm around midday.
They couldn't be contacted by anybody and the sergeant
had dispatched an engineer to repair the line.

At ten past four, I gave the signal to move in. Just
before I left the policia, they called me back, my wife
wanted me on the phone. She had been out, and returning,
she got my message that I wouldn't be home for the night.

music of a steel-band. And I shall admit: it took a long time but it was worth waiting for.

When I reached the stairs, I met Sergeant Munos, climbing, out of breath.

" Sir, the sergeant is on the phone from Elizondo. They've picked up The Smuggler."

Oh, Lord, let him bring good news! You remember all those promises I made, I'll keep them all and more, I'll keep Lent, I'll go to Lourdes, to Rome, I won't go to the bullfight, not even this year, I'll be faithful to my wife and give up Teresa-the-mare, and Rosana, my mistress, and I'll buy you a thousand candles. . . .

4

THE WHOLE AFTERNOON Father Esteban had been watering the flower-beds, ever since five o'clock that is, ever since the sun progressed behind the seminary walls so that the pink oleanders, the yellow roses, the pastel-red begonias, the golden brown azaleas crawled into their shadow. When he saw me in the window, he waved and I waved back to him. He got up every morning at four to water his flowers but to-day he did it a second time, so that they wouldn't die of thirst while he was away as he could not look after them during the whole of Saturday and most of Sunday. He made elaborate arrangements for his flowers, had explained to many of us how to set the sprinklers, how to soak the young plants in the steaming glass-house, and had been most apologetic when I reminded him that I, too, was one of his lucky fellow-priests who had been selected to take part in our week-end pilgrimage to Lourdes. There were six of us, all from the seminary, making up the batch

68

of this week-end's quota of pilgrims. For many years now, the authorities had allowed six priests to go every week-end and the four hundred odd priests of Pamplona took turns during the summer months. I had received my passport in April, last week an exit visa had been stamped on it. The abbot's secretary took it to the French Consulate, together with five others and brought it back with a French stamp in it. We had cheap railway fares on the Spanish railways and pilgrim's fare in France. For weeks now I had found it impossible to sleep and when I did, I dreamed of soft throbbing of trains, dreamy bleat of railway engines, strange French station names, the darkness of Lourdes' subterranean cathedral and the glow surrounding the Blessed Virgin's hair. Father Xavier, who shared my cell, often complained about my fitful tossing that kept him awake, but in the morning he usually smiled and told me of his own pilgrimages. Before the civil war, priests would go every year, often by chartered bus, it took only half an hour to Elizondo and another half an hour to Dancharinea and you were in France. Once across the border, you had many roads to choose from. You could take the fast road to Bayonne, the bus would race to Pau in an hour and from there in twenty minutes to Lourdes. Or you could travel via Oloron, or you could cross the border at Valcarlos, or possibly at Urdos. Father Xavier had travelled all these routes before the war, one did not need exit permits, not even visas. Nowadays pilgrims had to go by rail and had to be back thirty-six hours later. None of us young priests cared. I had never been out of Spain, I read much about travelling and I read everything I could lay my hands on about Lourdes. But, to be truthful, I couldn't quite imagine how it really would be. I used to pester the older priests with interminable questions and I was sure that

one of the reasons why Father Xavier agreed so easily to
represent me at the hospital, had been to escape my endless
inquisitiveness. Our party had to be ready by ten at night,
when the seminary car would take us to the station to catch
the train to Irun. I had packed my small bag days ago,
changing its contents from time to time, Father Xavier
had taken over my duties and now I had nothing to do but
wait and watch Father Esteban watering the flowers. Lucky
Father Esteban, for him time must be flying, he had so
much to think of, so many things to provide for his flowers,
while I stood at the open window, excited like a schoolboy,
looking at my watch every ten minutes, doubting that these
four hours will ever pass, feeling a little bit ashamed of
myself, allowing emotions to get the better of self-control,
emotions that I would not let get out of hand on any other
occasion, but which had got out of control like a benevolent
mob on a national holiday, with the police turning their
heads the other way.

At six p.m. a call came from the hospital, somebody was
asking for a priest. I was glad to accept Father Xavier's
offer to take over my duties earlier than it had been
intended. I felt that facing suffering, possibly even facing
death, would not be right in my present elated state of mind,
it would be almost indecent. So it shook me considerably
when Father Xavier returned an hour or so later and told
me that an old woman, with one foot obviously in the grave,
and who had up to now refused to see a priest, now
expressed a wish to see none other but me.

" Who is she?" I asked.

" Bed 24, along the wall, tiny face full of wrinkles. I hear
she has refused a blood transfusion."

I remembered her well. She had been pointed out to me
on Wednesday, but though I spoke to her, she refused to

answer, she just looked at me with hate in her eyes. I knew this look. I had seen it often in the eyes of agnostics. Godless, left-wing demagogues, who doubted the Lord, loved darkness better than light. Why did she change her mind? Father Xavier could not enlighten me on that. He had attended to the woman occupying bed 21, the lung-cancer case, who had been asking for a priest. He told me what had happened.

"After I had finished with No. 21 the matron spoke to me. Actually she had been inquiring about you, asking me to wish you a happy trip to Lourdes, hoping that you would say a prayer for her. Then a nurse came to say that No. 24 wished to have a priest. The matron got rather excited since the patient had not opened her mouth for days. She rushed away, presumably to call the doctor and I went over to the patient. Before I could say a single word, she told me that she wanted nothing to do with me. It was *you,* she wished to see. Only *you.* I must say: not very flattering."

Father Xavier's words left me in a slight confusion. Patients at the hospital often begged the priest to stay with them for hours and I did it gladly, knowing that they had derived solace from it. But to-night it was different. The clock had just struck seven. Getting to the hospital took at least twenty minutes, getting back the same. If that old woman suddenly found God and wanted to thrash out all her problems with God's representative on earth, it might take a long, long time. Still, it had to be done. In a way, it was a tribute to me. Had the old woman watched me talking to other patients yesterday? Had I been able to start her off on the road which led her back to God?

Of course I had to go.

I took the bus, the driver slowed down in front of the

travel bureau on the square, I jumped out and hurried towards the Calle de la Cruz. A car came from the other end of the street, stopping in front of the house opposite the hospital. Then another car arrived at the same destination. It struck me as strange. Never in the evening had I seen a car come to that house, though cars used to park there during visiting hours, but now it was much too late for that. I went inside the hospital. Two men stood up from the stone bench under the stairs. Though neither of them approached me, I could see both looking towards the porter's lodge as if encouraging the porter to speak to me. To my surprise it was still the day porter and when he came out to greet me, I remarked on this. He asked me to wait, went back to his lodge and, opening the small door to the back of it, he seemed to report my arrival to someone. Immediately, a head appeared in the door and I heard him saying:

" What, another priest?"

The porter explained: " This is the regular padre. The one before was only a replacement."

" Why a replacement if he's around himself?"

" Don't ask me," said the porter. " Priests are coming and going here all day."

" What for?" insisted the man, showing more of himself. " I have to report him, I don't see why they need two priests."

The porter resented this. " When you're about to turn up your toes, you always remember your Maker." The stranger shrugged and went back into the store room. A second later, I heard him cranking the house telephone and the porter telling him my name. In the meantime, the other two settled on the stone bench again, eyeing me with curious eyes. Then the porter came back and said that I might go upstairs.

"What's happening here?" I asked him, and he pulled a face, obviously disapproving of the proceedings.

"They think there is an epidemic case in one of the wards." He sent a furtive look towards the two under the stairs and added: "Be careful, Father."

While I had been climbing the stairs, it ran through my head, what do I do if this epidemic proved to be true? They might keep me here, or they might put me into quarantine. I might even catch it. I have never been ill and so I had no natural resistance for any disease. When I turned into the women's ward, I saw another stranger, staring down at me from the landing above. Who on earth are these people I had never seen before? Are they from the health authorities? The city's medical department?

When I entered the women's ward, someone had just closed the door of the nurses' rest-room and I could have sworn it was a man. The matron joined me, her face worried, she apologised for disturbing me in my preparations for the trip. She took me to bed No. 24, telling me that after giving the woman the sacrament, someone wished to speak to me. The little nurse pushed a chair close to the bed and I sat down.

"I'm Father Francisco," I began. "How do you feel?"

The old woman stared and said nothing. She had clear yellow eyes like a bird of prey. Her skin was dry and translucent, similar to old parchment. Her face was tiny, and hairy, with a thousand wrinkles as if the parchment had been folded in an erratic way and then opened out again. Without moving her head, her eyes wandered towards the matron and, in a croaky voice, she said:

" Send her away."

The matron understood and withdrew. The woman gave me another long stare, it made me feel uncomfortable. At long last she croaked again.

" I'm a heathen."

She waited for my reaction. I took her limp, dehydrated hand into mine. She drew it away at once as if from burning fire. " I'm going to die," she announced.

" We all do," I said. " The Lord giveth and taketh."

" Mostly taketh," she sneered. " Do you know who I am?"

I explained to her that the custom was not to ask for names. Before God we were all alike. She beckoned me to come closer and as she bent her finger, she was unable to straighten it again. When my ear almost touched her parched lips, she whispered:

" You are supposed to comfort the sick. Does your God care to grant an old woman's last wish?"

" God wants to grant every wish, if it is righteous."

A glimmer of comfort seemed to rise in her. Her hand groped after mine, but stopped short of it. Her whisper sounded for the first time void of suspicion.

" They want to kill my son. I want to save him."

" Who wants to kill your son?"

" Everyone here. They know he will come to see me. But I'm dying. If I'm dead, it's not worthwhile for him to take the risk."

The effort was wearing her out. I felt now her hand touching mine. I tried to find the right words. " Let me give you the sacrament," I said. " It'll ease your mind."

She shook her head.

" I don't want your sacrament. I want you to warn my son. Viñolas's men will kill him. They are waiting for him. Lurking in every corner."

She did not sound desperate, but rather cold and calculating, weighing up the chances, confiding in me since there was no one else to confide in. I said the only thing I could say. " I can't do anything against the police. I can't break the law."

" Whose law do you priests follow? God's law, or Viñolas's?" She was panting as if she had climbed a mountain and realised that she had taken the wrong route and had to retreat to take another. She paused before she spoke again. " Promise to warn my son. Promise to save his life and I'll take your sacrament. I make a deal with you. You warn him and I will submit to your hocus-pocus."

I shook my head. " I don't know who your son is, or what he did. But I can't make a deal."

Suddenly, with a jerk, she pulled my hand and kissed it. It was unexpected and it shook me with its savagery in body and soul. She went on mumbling. " You're a priest, have mercy on me and save my son." The rest of her words were lost in an inarticulate jabber. I'm afraid I must have looked utterly confused and I admit I greeted the appearance of the matron with relief. She took the woman's pulse, the wrinkled hand looked now whiter than the sheet. The matron announced, " She's in a coma," and, turning to a nurse who had hurried to help, " call Dr. Martinez." The nurse went to carry out the order. A man, the same man whose face I had seen in the rest-room door, came to join us.

" Did she talk about her son?" he asked. I nodded, still in a daze. The man took my arm and led me to the exit. " I'm Lieutenant Zapater from the guardia. You know, I suppose, who her son is?" I did not and I did not wish to know. There was one thing I wanted to do, to be alone. But the lieutenant shook his head. " Not now, Father. We need you. Captain Viñolas wants to speak to you."

We came down the stairs, traversed the hall, I caught a glimpse of the porter watching us passing with astonishment. I brushed off the lieutenant's hand still holding my arm. He held it not the way he would hold a prisoner, just giving me support. The lights were on in the hall and also in the street. We crossed to the opposite side and he led me into the house in front of which I had observed that unusual activity earlier.

What was this house that I had passed so often before without suspecting anything sinister about it, and why am I being taken to Captain Viñolas? Why did he wish to see me and why here, and not at the policia where I knew his office to be? Though I had never come face to face with him, I knew his name, everybody in Pamplona did. Once he came to the seminary to interrogate Father Esteban, after that horrible experience of his when that monster of a bandit broke into Father Esteban's church and when the guardia, together with carabineros of the whole of Navarra, were trying to pick up a clue to trace him. We were told that Viñolas sat for two days at Father Esteban's bedside, grilling him, very much against doctor's orders, without being able to get any sense out of the old man. Ever since, Father Esteban had been frail and somewhat feeble-minded and no one quite knew whether the encounter with that brigand or the experience with Viñolas had caused this indelible mark on his mind.

A carabinero stood guard at the bottom of the stairs, another had been posted in the ante-room. Lieutenant Zapater knocked and entered the inner sanctum, leaving me to wait outside. Though mention of the guardia made one's flesh creep in Spain, the clergy were even mightier. I felt no fear, the clergy and the guardia civil stood on the same side. Besides, I had done nothing against the law. But, it shot into my mind, I was just about to do just that. If he should ask me to repeat what the old woman said, I certainly would not. Bringing me here had obviously something to do with her and with her son, whoever he turned out to be. I couldn't disclose the contents of a confidential talk to anyone. No man of the clergy could. What the old woman entrusted me with was no different from a confession and as such, sacred. I felt no fear but it worried me what Viñolas would ask me and what I would answer him. The far more important implication of my experience hadn't occurred to me at that moment. When it did, I had no time to think, for the door had been opened and I was called inside.

Under stress, one's mind works faster, the senses become

more efficient, the eye sees sharper, the ear hears far above par. Though only a small light illuminated the room, I realised immediately that it had been transformed quite recently into this temporary office. The most startling object in the room was a large revolver on the desk, just outside the cone of light behind which sat Viñolas himself.

"You are Father Francisco," began the chief of police. He sounded benevolent. I again had the feeling of being on the same side with him, together with the forces which opposed law-breakers in the country. "You live in the seminary and you have been called into the hospital to talk to Pilar Artiguez."

"Artiguez?" I repeated foolishly as if I hadn't heard it clearly.

"Didn't you know?" Viñolas asked.

"No, I had no idea. I never ask for names. In fact, I don't want to know their names."

He watched me as a cat watches a bird which, flying off, is suddenly out of reach and cannot be followed.

"Well, you know now," he said. "She is the mother of Manuel Artiguez. You know him. The killer who desecrated the holy church." He paused, deciding how much he ought to tell me. I must have passed his scrutiny, for he continued: "I have set a trap. It is imperative that no one suspects it. That's why we are keeping the hospital sealed. You understand. . . ." He gave me a confidential smile. "I know that I can trust you, Father. The clergy and the guardia are on the same side. We both wish to clean up the country. You with prayers, we with enforcing the law. Tell me, did she say anything about her son?"

"You know that I can't tell you what she said."

His eyes bored into mine. "Every citizen must help to apprehend the enemies of the State, Father."

" If you force me to disclose what I shouldn't, you're no better than he who desecrated the church."

I saw him working it out for himself whether he should carry it a step farther. He was bluffing and so was I.

" I'm not forcing you to anything, Father. I hope you know where your duty lies."

I told him I did. He nodded several times, stood up to signify that the session had ended, when the phone rang. He answered it.

" Bring him up!" He turned to Lieutenant Zapater. " The Smuggler at last!" He held out his hand and while I shook it, he concluded: " I want you to promise not to tell anyone what is going on, what you have seen in the hospital, or here. It's essential. Come in, Carlos! What the hell has kept you?" He focused all his attention on the door, through which a young man entered, breathless from climbing the stairs, carrying a pack on his back, young, smooth, good-looking, with jet-black eyes and jet-black hair, greedy and knowing his worth, tired but grinning while unloading his pack.

" Not to-night," he announced. Viñolas stared at him, deflated, disappointed.

" What happened?"

Carlos let his pack fall on the sofa and came forward.

" He's too cautious. Too afraid. I told you his nerves have gone. But he *will* come. He wants me to find out the latest about Pilar. If she's not better, he'll be here to-morrow, Saturday."

" Where's he now?" asked Viñolas. " I've got everything ready for him."

Carlos shrugged his shoulders. " Still in the flat in Pau, 45 Spanish Street. He won't budge from there till

I return. He hopes I'll bring the news that she's better and he won't have to come."

Viñolas remembered me. " All right, Father. Lieutenant Zapater will take you downstairs." The telephone rang again and there was some commotion on the stairs. While Viñolas coped with the call, a man in mufti burst in.

" Sir!" he called, and there was doom in his hollow voice. " She has died!"

His chief must have heard the same shattering report on the phone, for he held his breath, needing time to collect himself. Then he inhaled a mouthful of the thick, smoky air, put down his cigarette and missed the ash-tray. You could see his hand shaking in the circle of light on the desk. At last he said into the phone: " I'll be over in a minute. Don't let anybody in or out. And don't let anybody touch her!" He replaced the receiver and repeated for the sake of those present: " She has died."

The Smuggler, called Carlos, swore blasphemously, Lieutenant Zapater took the receiver from the desk, where his chief had left it and replaced it where it belonged, the man in mufti mumbled: " I'm sorry, sir." I stood there not knowing whether I could leave, whether a move towards the door would draw their attention unnecessarily to me, with quite the opposite result of what I hoped to achieve, to melt away out of this room, where I heard so much I did not wish to know. Gradually Viñolas came to life. Only in men who are used to reverses, does one find such resilience. He weighed up the situation, appraised the facts, and began to draw logical conclusions. If one acted quickly and resolutely, nothing was lost yet. Pilar's death was a great blow. Still for a short time—for twenty-four hours certainly—one could keep it secret. Visitors could be barred for another day. One could maintain the fraud of a suspected contagious disease for twenty-four hours longer. No outsider had left the hospital and no one would. Carlos would have to return to Pau at once, a police car would take him to the border, to-morrow morning he would be in Pau. He must convince Manuel of the urgency to come over. He must say that he had seen Pilar, that she was sinking steadily, that the doctors gave her only a couple of days at the most, and that she was asking for her son.

" Say what you like but get him over! You can count on an extra twenty thousand if you succeed, Carlos!"

Lieutenant Zapater ordered a car for Carlos, his chief hurried over to the hospital, Carlos loaded his pack on his back. Orders were barked to prevent the news getting outside.

But I was forgotten and I *was* outside. Nobody bothered to stop me when I descended the stairs and stepped into the sultry night.

A small voice in my breast said: You mustn't do anything. But a big voice demanded: You must! The small voice winced: How can you? You can never get in touch with him. The big voice boomed: You know his name, you know where he can be found, you are going to Lourdes, Pau is only a short distance from Lourdes. I thought, this time hopefully: I have missed the train. But the clock over the entrance to the bank showed only twenty past eight.

I am a priest and cannot be involved in defrauding the law. I stepped down from the pavement, the huge laundry-van swerved, the face of an angry driver appeared in the window to curse me, but seeing my garb, he just shook his head and said: " God forgive you!"

I doubted that God would forgive me. I had forsaken

a dying woman for sheer lack of patience with her. Who was I to be her judge? Her motive could not be more righteous, more noble: she wished to save her son. She did not believe in religion and, still, she offered to accept the sacrament. She offered to give up her principles in order to snatch her child from the jaws of death. And what did I do? Haughtily, I turned her down. Like some bank manager who turns down a loan because he does not fancy the security offered. I looked up at the bank, its shutters down, sure and secure and soulless.

A bus slowed down in front of me, the driver thought I was waiting to board it. I started for it but when I saw its number, number 45, I turned away. Number 45, number 45 Spanish Street, that's what Carlos said. There lived a man for whom machine-guns were waiting in Pamplona. His dead mother was waiting for him, too. They were using his dead mother as bait.

I walked towards the travel bureau and joined the queue at the bus stop. The shop window blazed with lights. Huge, sharp photographs of Lourdes, with a banner across them: *Visitez* Lourdes! The City of the Blessed Virgin! *Visitez* Lourdes! (O, Blessed Virgin, make me do the right thing!) Another display urged: *Visitez* Pau! Its Château! Its *Boulevard des Pyrénées*! I studied the painted map of the Pyrénées stuck to the inside of the window. The places I had been dreaming of were all there: Irun, San Sebastian, Bayonne, Pau and Lourdes, I found them all.

I got back to the seminary with only a few minutes to spare. They were waiting for me, had already phoned the hospital and sent Father Anselmo to look for me. I fetched my bag and, finding Father Xavier in our cell, I asked him:

" Do you remember whether you and matron discussed

my going to Lourdes in the presence of that old woman?"

He had forgotten already. "What old woman?"

"The woman who insisted on speaking to me."

"Oh, that one! I suppose we did mention it. In fact I'm certain matron did mention it. Why? Don't tell me she wanted to see you to ask you to pray for her to the Blessed Virgin."

"I won't," I said, but a second later I was sorry for being so high-handed and apologised.

"Well, say one for me," he asked. I promised and told him that the old woman had died.

"Did she? I hope you arrived in time?"

"I did."

"Well, that's all right then," he said. "I hope that your trip will be a wonderful experience for you. And I hope you'll sleep better when you get back."

He did not come downstairs to join those who crowded round the bus to wave good-bye. He wanted to go to bed and make up for lost sleep of the last few nights.

Many came, all the cell-mates were there, including the abbot and his secretary. The driver of the small bus switched on the light inside, revved up his engine, the lights dipped and came on again, the secretary checked with Father Erasmus if he had our passports, our tickets, our food. There were shouts: "See you on Sunday! Have a wonderful time! Keep together!" The whole scene had a strange picnic spirit, it reminded me of the careless days of my childhood when our school went on its annual excursion, one year to Zaragoza, another to Burgos, and when I mentioned it to Father Esteban who sat at my side, he remembered having been in Zaragoza himself on a pilgrimage as a young priest, he thought it was in October and the pilgrimage was called "*La Virgen del Pilar*".

"You must, one day, do the pilgrimage of Pilar." And when I said that I was doing it now, they looked at me as if *I* had been slightly off balance and not Father Esteban.

I wrote: "Dear Manuel Artiguez." At Irun, I changed it to: "Dear Señor." At Hendaye, I altered it to: "Dear Mr. Artiguez," at Bayonne, I modified it to: "Manuel Artiguez." But the text remained the same. "You don't know me, I had a chance of speaking to your dear mother, Pilar, before she died and promised her to let you know her last wish: do not come to Pamplona. She died with your name on her lips and anxiety in her heart for her son." I signed it: "A friend." I had bought a packet of writing-paper at the station at Pamplona and spent almost all the money I had on it. The packet contained 24 sheets and 10 envelopes. My plan was to mail my letter at the station at Pau. They were bound to deliver it during the day, I had heard the French postal service was very fast and efficient, much more efficient than ours in Spain. I wrote in semi-darkness, sitting in the corner of the compartment, the lights had been turned down, everybody being asleep except Father Esteban. I didn't have to worry about him. He sat opposite me, smiling his usual little smile, watching without seeing, and dreaming with open eyes all through the night, while our train sped through the Spanish landscape and then through the French. When at last I had finished my writing, I asked him:

"Why don't you sleep?"

His smile turned gentler. "I can't. I'm too excited."

"You must try."

He shook his head. "I can't. You don't sleep either."

"I had to finish this letter. I want to mail it in Pau."

He nodded as if he had understood that one had to write

letters and one had to mail them in Pau. "And *I* have a lot to think about. I shall take the holy bath in the holy spring, so that I shall get better."

He said this rather cheerfully and it sounded so much more desperate, so much more heartbroken that it made me almost cry. I whispered: "There is nothing in the world the matter with you."

He chuckled again in his own vague way. "Oh, yes, there is. Don't you know that I'm barmy? Ever since that night in my church."

I stroked his tunic. "Don't talk about it."

"But I want to talk about it."

"You mustn't. It upsets you."

He was lost again, staring out of the window, not following what I had said at all, not even knowing that I was there. Ahead of us the sky looked like deep-green blotting paper, the lower edge of which, well out of sight, had been immersed in a purple juice, which now lazily oozed upwards.

I wondered what might be going on in his moonstruck mind ever since it had been swept clean by the cruel broom of that terrible night. Why did he smile all the time? He didn't before, I remembered well, he used to be rather a querulous old bird, looking after the accounts of the seminary, punctilious and somewhat pompous. But since that ghastly experience, he wished to have nothing to do with accounts, he seemed suddenly to have acquired an infallible way to grow and tend flowers. Like a Pied Piper, he just stood and smiled and plants broke through the soil to come to him. I wondered what he thought of his attacker and what he would say if he knew that I was trying to save him. What would his reaction be if he knew that when the train stopped in the station at Pau, he was only a short distance away from Manuel Artiguez? And what, if the two happened to come face to face?

The purple juice had spread over the eastern sky and now a pale yellow, followed by golden-white, surged up in the wake of it. The first rays of the rising sun hit Father Erasmus, very appropriately I thought, for he had been our appointed leader, the only one who spoke a few words of French. And was he proud of it! He held the few coins of French currency we had been given by the secretary in case something unforeseen happened. He knew the French words for " pilgrim ", for " train ", he could count up to a hundred and, as soon as we had left Pamplona, he started a free course in practical French. But when I asked him to tell me the French word for " letter-box ", he got irritated and refused to tell me.

" You don't want to have anything to do with letter-boxes. We don't want to spend money on stamps."

" I want to mail a letter in France," I argued. " And now that you remind me, I also need a stamp. What is ' stamp ' in French?"

He shook his head resolutely and pocketed the pocket dictionary which had been given to him, no doubt, for the use of all six of us. Suddenly I had several supporters and he was obliged to produce the dictionary. I made notes of several words which would help me to buy a stamp and find the box to mail it. He made a remark vaguely suggesting that the fact of mailing a letter in France meant that I had friends among Spanish exiles and this was just as improper as spending church money on postage stamps. I carried my point, but I had to bear with his disapproval and small bickerings for the whole blessed night. He turned away from me and addressed Father Esteban.

" Where are we?"

But Father Esteban did not hear, just smiled and stared out of the window. So I said, as a peace-offering: "We have passed through a place called Orthez."

To show that he had not forgotten any of my sins, he did not answer. He took the dictionary from his pocket and began to study it. From the corridor came the noise of sliding doors and the conductor's voice, announcing that the train was just about to stop at Pau, came closer. I spoke to Father Erasmus again: "I wonder if you would be good enough to ask the conductor how long we are stopping at Pau?"

He looked up then, turning his attention back to the dictionary, he said: "I will ask him when he comes." When he did come, Father Erasmus got flustered, mumbled a shy question which the conductor couldn't understand and gave it up, blushing in defeat, angry to have revealed to us the limitations of his linguistic competence. The arrival of the conductor and the short dialogue between him and Father Erasmus had woken up everybody. This made our leader even more resentful.

"He is not familiar with my accent," he declared.

Father Anselmo stretched his numb limbs, telling us what a wonderful sleep he had had. Father Vicente wiped his face with a handkerchief, examining it carefully.

"What blessing, these electrified railway lines. You can open the windows without getting to look like chimney-sweeps."

The rails ran here in a deep ravine. The steep bank had green turf, oval-shaped flower-beds, tall palm-trees, and just before reaching the block-house, I discovered a funicular leading up to the heart of the town. I would have thought Father Esteban would be interested in the flowers, but he turned away from the window and said:

"I'm thirsty. Can you get something for me?" He addressed Father Erasmus, remembering his leading position among us. Father Erasmus passed the request on to me.

"Father Francisco will do it. I don't think you can get water here. But perhaps some fruit juice. Something not too expensive."

He searched for the appropriate coin among his French money and handed it to me. I got up, stepped over their legs, and went out to the corridor. The train had slowed down and slid smoothly, with its slightly pulsating motion, over points, crossing clusters of parallel lines. I felt for the letter in my pocket. Quite a number of people were getting out, lining up at both ends of the corridor, clutching their luggage, some leaning out of the windows calling for porters. I saw the door of our compartment pushed aside and Father Esteban came out to join me.

"I'll come with you," he said.

"No, you mustn't. You watch me from here," I pleaded with him. He smiled his endearing smile.

"I don't really want a drink," he announced. "God be with you."

The train stopped. For a second I stood in the surging tide of an uncharted sea of people. I asked a porter struggling to drag a suitcase through a window. "*Lettre. Timbre. Timbre for lettre.*" I showed him my letter and when he understood he nodded towards the bookstall. I raced to the bookstall. "*Timbre,*" I called to the girl behind mountains of newspapers and gory magazines, holding up my letter in pantomime. She asked a question I did not understand, leaned forward to read the address.

"Ah, Pau," she said, "*deux sous, mon père.*" She gave me the stamp, took Father Erasmus's coin from my palm

and handed back some small change. Encouraged by her
kindness, I asked : " *Boîte aux lettres?*" She leaned forward
once more, pointing along the platform.

" *Deuxième porte, mon père. Voila, le facteur.*"

I saw the postman who had just emptied the box and
was leaving the platform and sprinted after him. I caught
him in the ticket hall, held out my letter, pleading with him
in Spanish. " Please take it, it's very important." But the
postman shook his head, pointed back to the platform,
indicating that he had no right to collect letters the way
I suggested, and I had to mail it the proper way. From the
platform, I heard the banging of doors and the sickly smooth
gliding of the departing train. In my terror, I left the postman and ran back to the platform. The train was gone.
I stood in panic staring after it as it gathered speed, turning
slightly, then straightening out again, my terror growing
as its faraway din was waning. Two porters joined me to
commiserate, asking sympathetic questions which I could
not answer, not having understood them. They took me
to a huge board on which the times of departing trains
were indicated, to show me that an hour later another train
was leaving for Lourdes, shortly afterwards another—in
fact, every hour there was a train leaving for Lourdes. I
could not and would not tell them that Father Erasmus had
my ticket. I imagined the commotion among my friends.
Father Anselmo wanting to pull the communication cord,
Father Erasmus protesting in case one had to pay a fine,
but, in truth, being afraid to have to talk again to the
conductor who did not understand his French accent, and
everybody worrying about me, having no money and no
ticket.

I had the letter in my hand and asked the two porters
about the Spanish Street. They called another colleague

and he called another. They consulted each other, drew into their conference a railway guard with dramatic gestures, they borrowed from the girl at the bookstall a guide-book of Pau, but could not find a Spanish Street in the index. Then a man buying a morning paper heard them and he knew where the street was. He knew that its proper name was Rue Soumoulou, he spoke a little Spanish and explained how to get there. You had to go up the funicular, cross the Place Royal, turn right into the Rue Maréchal Joffre which becomes Rue Maréchal Foch and then the Cours Bosquet. There I should ask again.

The nice girl at the bookstall watched my embarrassment about the funicular, saw me counting my French coins, took the letter from my hand, tore off the stamp and, with a smile, handed me back the money I had paid for it. They followed me outside, put me into the funicular, talked to the conductor who refused to take money from me, then he blew a penny-whistle and we were off. We climbed slowly up the track cut into the hillside among tall palms planted on the steep bank and when we were level with their tops, we had reached the Boulevard des Pyrénées. It was a lofty, fine boulevard, with a view of the mountains, some of their peaks snow-capped. Somewhere behind them was Pamplona and Viñolas, the hospital, and the whole gruesome business. The boulevard looked very much like the picture on the poster I had seen in the window at the bus stop near the hospital in Pamplona. Only the pretty girl who, on the poster, gazed towards the mountains was missing. I found the Place Royal, crossed it, passing in front of a travel bureau advertising: *Visitez Pamplune! Pamplune* must be Pamplona in French, for I recognised the cathedral, an exaggerated version of our ayuntamiento, the ancient ramparts and, of course, the Plaza de Toros. I discovered without difficulty the two streets named after famous French generals, asked with the help of my well-tried pantomime how to get to Rue Soumoulou, it again caused a public inquiry till a man with a Basque beret pronounced that there was a Rue of the name I mentioned but everybody called it Spanish Street. This information was greeted with general approval for here everyone knew of the Spanish Street. They showed me how to get there safely, they showed me how to get there fast and how to get there fastest and, eventually, I found it: a narrow lane with Spanish names over the shops. The grocer stood outside his business cursing a bunch of children whose football had fallen into a barrel of pickled olives which stood at the entrance to his shop. I stopped and he greeted me with reverence, like a man would greet a priest in Spain. I asked him how far Lourdes was by road and calculated that I could do it in seven hours for certain. I could be there not later than 4 p.m. and I would still have a little time left.

Now there was nothing else to do but find the house, number 45, and that was easy. I felt fine, the feeling of panic had left me, I knew that I was meant to come here and, having arrived, nothing could go wrong.

WHEN I GROW UP I'll marry a woman like Monique. It is true the Silent Woman knows more about chickens and ducks and cooking and she stands behind her husband to serve him at meals, but I won't have chickens and ducks in my backyard, and I shall like the company of my wife at the table. Also, I wouldn't like her to get up at dawn to feed the fowls, to milk the cows and open the gate for them. I'd like to smell the scent of her pyjama-top and on Saturdays and Sundays stay in bed till nine and talk with her how to spend the week-end, whether to take the car and go somewhere, whether we should go to a place in the mountains and have trout for lunch, and whether we should take our swimming things—just like Antonio and Monique talk on Saturday morning, or on Sunday morning before they get out of bed.

It came as a surprise to me to be woken up by a clatter in the kitchen and to see by my watch that it was only a quarter to eight. Had I mistaken the day? Not likely. It was Friday yesterday, so it must be Saturday to-day. Well, I could find out for myself. I could go into the kitchen, pretending that I wanted a glass of water and ask Monique. Perhaps it was she who had forgotten the day and I would tell her so, and she would laugh about her foolishness, thank me for telling her, and go back to bed beside Antonio, who would go on smelling the scent of her pyjama-top. Lucky fellow, Antonio, I thought. If he had been a rascal, I wouldn't have minded. But he wasn't. Perhaps, being a good man had its compensations. The life of a rascal was exciting, so he needed no compensations. But the life of a good man was dull, so good men were given wives like Monique to make up for the dullness so that he could smell the scent and snuggle up to his wife under the warm blanket.

Monique had bought me two pairs of pyjamas, one with thin green stripes, another with blue stripes. In the shop she said that she couldn't understand why no one made only pyjama-tops, without the pants, as most people wore only the tops and to buy pants was just a waste of money and material. I wondered what I would do now if I had no trousers to mine, I certainly couldn't go into the kitchen and face her without them. I combed my hair to look reasonably well so early in the morning, and practised the thirsty look in the mirror so that she would believe that I had come only for a glass of water. I opened the kitchen door and found not her, but Antonio, making coffee.

" Hallo, Pablo," he said. " Want some coffee?"

" It's Saturday," I muttered.

" I know it's Saturday. We're working at the factory till lunch-time. Something urgent. I thought I'd let Monique have her Saturday snooze."

He was completely dressed. I watched him pouring boiling water over the powdery coffee. He used much less coffee than Monique, probably because he was a good man.

Rascals used much more coffee and it tasted better. Perhaps Monique was a rascal, too, and that was what made me like her so much.

" I promised Monique to take out the car after lunch," Antonio said. " We'll show you round."

I wondered what he meant by taking out the car as it stood in front of the house the whole blessed day. I said yes, and he asked me why I wasn't more enthusiastic about it and I assured him that I was very enthusiastic and then

he wanted to know how I got on with learning French.
Always, when he disliked what I said, or did, he brought
up my learning French. I replied that I made excellent
progress and he asked: " How do you say ' black ' in
French?" I admitted that I had not got as far as that,
" black " being one of those words I would not use very
often and he said, what would I say to a waiter in a bistro
if I wanted to order black coffee? I told him that I wouldn't
order black coffee, since I preferred white coffee, and he
said, why didn't you say so and got up to fetch some
milk, and I thought that from now I would have to drink
white coffee always though I liked black. But then he
asked me what " white " was in French and I didn't know
that either. He warned me not to go to the Spanish Street
too often and to play instead with French children, and
I promised. He told me that a month ago he repaired a
very old cabinet in the home of Manuel Alvarez, whom
people regarded as the most famous Spaniard in Pau, a
wholesale merchant, dealing in eggs and poultry. The
family had two children, both going to French schools,
speaking nothing but French just like any French child.
I said nothing, wondering how he could be so ignorant for
surely the other Manuel, the one I helped to memorise the
layout of that hospital in Pamplona, was the most famous
Spaniard in Pau. I had never heard of a man called Alvarez,
wholesale egg and poultry merchant before, but everybody
in the whole world has heard of Manuel Artiguez.

Antonio went on tiptoe so that Monique could sleep
undisturbed, but as soon as he closed the front door,
Monique called me. I had been in the bedroom before, but
this time it had not yet been made up and Monique was still
in bed. She said the front door banging had woken her

up and asked me if Antonio had gone? The blinds were still down, the windows were open, she smelt a mixture of flowers and grown-up woman.

"Sit down, Pablo. Here on the bed. These pyjamas do suit you. Which one is this?"

I swallowed and said it was the green one.

"You had coffee with Antonio?" she asked.

I just nodded. I wanted to say that she was the most beautiful woman I had ever seen and that I would marry someone like her if I could ever find her, that I would keep our secret till eternity, no torture of Viñolas could ever drag it out of me. But I said only: "Your coffee is better than Antonio's."

She laughed, each one of her white teeth laughed separately. It reminded me of the band playing at the bandstand on the Plaza del Castillo, the bandsmen playing different tunes on different instruments, but the whole coming out as one. She told me to get her purse from her bag. The bag smelt strongly scented and when I inhaled it, I almost fainted. She gave me three New-Francs to go to the cinema at 10.30, they had children's performances on Saturday morning. She thought Marcel might still be in town and might bring a new kind of wine to taste, but she knew that I was not very keen on wine in the morning, especially sweet wine. Neither was Antonio and he couldn't understand how people could drink it in the morning, and so she never mentioned it to him. She kissed me on the cheek, in spite of my holding a different view on sweet wine, and asked me if I wanted to use the bathroom now, or after her? Though I loved to bathe after her, I knew that she took a long time and I had promised Manuel—not the dealer in eggs and poultry—that I'd be there by nine o'clock to go over his notes on the hospital once more.

When I turned into the Spanish Street, the children were already there, kicking the crooked football for all they were worth. They took no notice of me. It was a deliberate snub to make me feel that I didn't exist so far as they were concerned. Someone kicked the ball right at me, I jumped over it and went on my way. One of these days, I'll show you how to play football, you big monkeys.

I climbed the stairs and knocked at the door. Immediately, as if he had been standing waiting for it, Manuel opened the door. He spoke in a whisper.

" Carlos has got in. He's sleeping."

He nodded towards the other room and told me, rather gloomily, that the news was bad.

" She's worse. And she wants to see me."

" Are you going?" I must have said it rather anxiously, for he got angry.

" What else can I do? Why are *you* so keen for me to go?"

I said that I was not keen at all, but he knew I was. He wanted to cross to-night and before to-night there was much to do. Pedro would arrive any minute now and together they would go to a secret place to get the " Thompsons ". I thought the Thompsons were brothers of some foreign extraction, however, they turned out to be submachine-guns buried in the young forest along the Gave, close to the road, but unknown to anybody. The plot of ground belonged to Pedro who had bought it years ago to build on, but never did. Pedro seemed very keen on land, owned property in many places and Manuel admired him for it. The patch of land also carried the

D

fishing rights on the adjoining part of the Gave. Most
people who owned land along the Gave let the Depart-
mental Fishing Agency hire it out to fishermen, but Pedro
kept the rights and put up large signs: " Fishing Strictly
Prohibited ". Not that Pedro relished fishing. He did it
on account of the Thompsons.

While Manuel thus spoke to me in a whisper, he watched
the street from the window, hoping to see Pedro arrive.
At last he said:

" I've got some shopping to do, I'll do it now to save
time. Can you stay here in case Pedro arrives?"

Of course I could stay. I was now part of the whole
secret operation, determined to play my part the best I
could. My chest was swelling with pride. If only The
Bicycle could see me, if only The Flute could hear how
Manuel Artiguez spoke to me, if only those silly boys and
girls on the street could watch me being entrusted with all
this confidential information. Holy smoke, there would be
gasps and battle-cries when they heard that I knew about it
all the time. Who had been right about Manuel? Even
Antonio will have to admit that Manuel is a great man
and Monique . . . She will know that she can trust me
with the greatest of secrets, since the bravest men had
trusted me and I did not breathe a word. Each time the
children toss a coin to pick teams for opposing sides, there
would be heated arguments over which team I was to play
for. I might say I didn't feel like playing at all with their
crooked ball, or I might even say: " I'll show you novices
what goal-keeping really is," and offer my three New-Francs
to anyone who could kick the ball past me in the whole
width of the street. And I might even say that di Stefano,
himself, had tried and hadn't succeeded in kicking a goal
against me, and they would believe it since they had

doubted what I said about Manuel Artiguez, too, and in the end they had had to eat their words. And, suddenly, I heard Manuel saying:

" I want to buy a present for you, Pablo. What would you say to a brand-new football?"

It was enough to take one's breath away. To be Manuel Artiguez's friend, to be a great goalkeeper and also to *own* the best football in the Spanish Street, that was really something one could hardly bear. Manuel mistook my astonishment for hesitation.

" Perhaps you'd rather have a pelota outfit?"

I started to hiccup and thanked him and said that there was no need to buy me a present, and I trembled with fright in case he should take me at my word. But he just hissed at me, reminding me that Carlos was resting in the next room and said that he had never known such a little idiot as me. I had rendered him good service and he never accepted any service without paying for it and I had to accept his present even if he had to force me to. If I chose the pelota outfit, he'd fasten the " chistera " on one of my ears. I told him that whatever this " chistera " might be, I resented it being fastened on my ear. He explained that the wicker-basket pelota players used on the hand was called a " chistera " and said that perhaps I knew nothing about football either, and I told him that I had been chosen four times for the school eleven, we lost only once and then only because the referee was a teacher from the opposing school.

" So, football it will be," he declared and went. If Pedro arrived, or Carlos woke up, I was to tell them that Manuel intended to be back not later than in half an hour, but I was to let Carlos sleep, for he had got in only about two hours ago having crossed the mountain in half the time, knowing that Manuel was anxiously awaiting his news.

I could hear Carlos snoring in the next room. On the whole I did not fancy snoring, it reminded me of Father Aloysius who taught religion in school. A big fat priest, with ruddy face, who let us copy psalms from the Bible and always fell asleep, sitting behind his desk, his head leaning on one of his arms, while the other arm he spread across the top of the desk, his huge hand resting on the inkstand, snoring away like lavatory gurgle. One morning The Bicycle brought a plateful of vegetables to class: carrots, turnips, an onion, spinach and a few leaves of lettuce. I thought he had brought them for the school rabbit, though I had never seen rabbits eating onions. He behaved very mysteriously and said that he wouldn't bother to bring things for rabbits since he disliked them. The greenery was meant for Father Aloysius. This did not make sense for we knew The Bicycle disliked priests even more than rabbits. Only later did we understand what he planned to do. When Father Aloysius fell asleep, The Bicycle crept up to him, with extreme care he lifted the enormous hand, not too high, only so that he could slide the plate under it. Then he set out to decorate the hand on the plate with vegetables. He was a master at it. He wedged carrots and turnips between the fleshy fingers, he put salad around them, the fingernails he decorated with spinach. Then he cut the onion in half and placed the halves right in front of Father Aloysius's trembling snozzle. The priest twitched his nose, made faces, while we were holding our sides and almost died with convulsive laughter. Then he slowly opened his piggy-eyes and saw the plateful of sausages, embellished with all that garnish and then he began to find those sausages slightly familiar and suddenly withdrew them, horror-stricken, uttering a fearful cry like a wounded rhinoceros. Oh, it was unforgettable.

Still, I didn't mind Carlos snoring. I loved Carlos though I had never seen him before. I loved him since he brought the news for Manuel which made him decide to go to Spain and be a hero again.

Still grinning about the memory of Father Aloysius, I went to the window, wondering in which shop Manuel would buy the football. There were lots of people in the street. Among them I saw a priest. He was different from all the holy men I had met in France. He looked to me like a Spanish priest. A strange, alarming feeling rose in me, I got, suddenly, very hot under the collar and started to hiccup. What if they had sent a priest from Spain to question me about that practical joke The Bicycle played on Father Aloysius? I watched him, terror-stricken, as he moved among the people, looking up at the numbers of houses, searching for the right one. My hands felt sticky, I wiped them and I dried my face, too. The priest disappeared under the shoemaker's sign, beneath the window and just above the entrance to the house. If only he would reappear again. If he would, he would pass on. But he didn't. He had entered the house. Of course he might have gone into the shoemaker's. I tiptoed to the hall and, with my burning ear to the door, I listened. I could hear his steps coming up the stairs. For a moment I wanted to run back and call Carlos, then I remembered all that Manuel had said about letting Carlos sleep since he had a hard night's climbing. The steps came higher and higher, closer and closer. Suddenly I saw the key in the door. Why hadn't I thought of turning the key before? I tried to turn it, first with one hand, then with both. It wouldn't turn. I pressed my fingers against that stupid key so that

it hurt. It refused to budge. By now I was in a panic.
I searched my pockets and whipped out a pencil, wedged
it into the key and tried to twist it. The pencil broke. I
wanted to push up the door handle, when he knocked and
I jumped back, with aching hands and smarting eyes and
stifled breath. The door opened slowly, the black vampire
was in the hall. He said good morning and asked if I was
Spanish? I said nothing, for I could not open my mouth
even if I had wanted to. He smiled at me. Perhaps spiders
smile, too, before they tie-up a fly.

"Does Manuel Artiguez live here?" He waited for an
answer and when I nodded, he closed the door and
advanced. I trembled with fear and still I hoped that he
would get away from the door. One more step and I would
dart forward, tear open that door and dive for the stairs.
He held up a letter. "I'm Father Francisco. I come from
Pamplona. I must see Mr. Artiguez."

Now I recognised him. I was quite certain I had seen
him going into the hospital and coming from it. He
wanted Manuel, not me. Well, Manuel could take care of
himself. The letter had Manuel's name written on it.
Gradually, I managed to collect my wits.

"He's out," I said.

He seemed very perturbed. "He didn't go to Spain?"
he asked.

I said nothing. Obviously he wanted to trick me into
telling him my secret. I wasn't having any of his tricks.

"It's very urgent. His life depends on it. I can't stay
here, I'm on my way to Lourdes. When is he coming
back?"

"I don't know." I wanted to be as non-committal as
possible.

"So he hasn't left for Spain yet?"

It *was* a trick. I knew it. I had to be on my guard. I fought now, not for myself but for my friend and partner, the great Manuel Artiguez. I, Pablo Dages, Defender of the Faith, Paladin against the dark forces of evil. Quite unexpectedly he played himself into my hands.

"Will you see him? Can you give him a message? Will you give him this letter?"

"I might."

"Look, tell him he mustn't go to Pamplona. His mother is dead. It was her last wish that he should not risk his life. Since she is dead, there is no sense in it."

Now I knew for certain that he was lying.

"Pilar is not dead," I said.

But he insisted that she was. He spoke to her yesterday, she passed away at eight o'clock last night.

"I implore you to find him and tell him what I have said. And give him this letter. I can't give you anything for your trouble, I've got nothing. Will you promise to do what I'm asking?"

I would have promised anything to get rid of him. So that was it, he wanted to cheat Manuel into staying away from Spain. Well, he won't succeed. But he mustn't meet Manuel, for Manuel was not very keen to go, the slightest reason might sway him against going. And then all these silly children would be right in calling him a coward and a mighty mouse. I told the priest that I would find Manuel and he said that he would pray for me so that I succeed in warning him. At long last, he was out of the flat. I went into the next room and listened to Carlos's snoring. I leant out of the window and saw Father Francisco walking down the street. Then I returned to the hall, grabbed the letter and took it to the lavatory. I tore it up, dropped the bits into the bowl and pulled the chain. The water

rushed up and washed away the pieces, all except one. On
that one I could read, in spite of the obliterating effect of
the water, "Your dear mother, Pilar." I pulled the chain
again in a frenzy, but with no effect since the tank was
empty and needed time to replenish. I seized the brush to
force it down the throat of the bowl with the result that it
got stuck on the bristles. I tried the chain and now a trickle
of water began to ooze, catching the last piece in its minia-
ture whirlpool, sucking it down. I left the lavatory, but
a strange, hissing noise made me turn. To my horror, in
the bowl's rising water, there were all the torn bits of the

letter. I caught the sound of the door opening in the hall, I banged down the lid, pulled the chain once more, and heard a familiar voice:

" Pablo, amigo."

It was Pedro, laughing, joking and telling me that he had brought love from the silent woman and also a cake. He would have come to see me at my uncle's, but things got rather pressing, time being short. He might have to drive Manuel to a plot of land along the Gave. He told me that he got up very early and saw a shooting star. As far as he was concerned nothing could mean better luck than seeing a shooting star in June just before sunrise.

I asked him: " Is meeting a priest bad luck, Pedro?"

" Not for me. Neither is it for Manuel. But it is bad luck for the priest."

He roared with laughter and I had to ask him to roar more quietly since Carlos slept in the next room and Manuel wanted him to rest for he had been on the road all night.

" These young puppies always get tired!" he said. " Tired of what? When I was young, I got tired only of one thing." He wouldn't say what that thing was and when I guessed that he meant pelota, he shook his head. He had got up this morning well before sunrise, but he didn't feel at all tired. The only thing he needed was to use the lavatory. I started to hiccup and he tried to stop it by patting me on the back, and suggested pouring cold water on the back of my head and I persuaded him to let me do it in the lavatory as one had to cross the bedroom where Carlos rested in order to get to the bathroom. He agreed. I went inside with thumping heart. Pedro followed me. I would have liked to peer under the lid. But Pedro gave me no chance. He turned on the tap and held my head under it. Being so occupied and happy that his remedy worked, he forgot his need.

I asked him: " Pedro, do priests ever tell the truth?"

" They might. In their dreams, perhaps. But I've never heard them."

I sighed with relief.

Shortly afterwards Manuel came back. He stopped outside the door, opened a chink in it and kicked my football through. It bounced between the legs of the table, ricocheted from the chest of drawers, jumped on the sofa, rebounded from the wall above it and landed in my arms. It already knew its master. It was a wonderful football, white with a greenish hue, soft and light, but not too light, laced as it should be and round. Not crooked like that thing the children of the Spanish Street called a football. While Manuel and Pedro shook hands and Manuel told his news about Pilar, I bounced my football up and down. There was no need to force its fall, you just drew away your hands, let it drop on its own, and up it came. I thanked Manuel and he winked at Pedro and told him how useful I had been and what a wonderful memory I had.

" Now, down you go and try it out with the boys. We have to talk, Pedro and I. I'll wake up Carlos." He dived into his pocket and produced a lacing-bodkin which the shopkeeper told him went with the football, and pushed me outside.

I went downstairs, but for a while stayed indoors. I could hear the children running after their crooked ball and imagined the imminent turmoil my appearance would produce among them. I enjoyed the moment of expectation and wanted to prolong it. I threw up my football just short of the landing and let it come down to me in easy bounces, once, twice, again and again. Then, suddenly, there was a rush outside and the crooked ball appeared, having lost its sense of direction, kicked somewhere where it shouldn't have been. It came to rest at my feet, next to my own gleaming treasure, as if ashamed of its lop-sided bounce in front of a real football. A second later a stocky little boy swept through the door after the ball. He raced

in, head down, like a bull running into the arena, decelerating suddenly and for a moment blinded by the contrast of light. When his eyes got adjusted to the dark, he discovered his ball, gasped at the sight of mine and stared at me, struck with awe. At last, he whispered:

" Is that yours?"

I nodded.

" May I hold it?"

I nodded again. He wiped his hands on his pants, picked

it up, taking no notice of the other ball, holding it gingerly,
panting from running and excitement.

" Does it bounce?" he asked.

" What do you think?" I challenged him.

He let it go and was just as much astonished by its
feather-light fall and rise as I was before. He grinned at
me in acknowledgment and bounced it once more. Now
another face appeared in the light of the door, that of the
ginger-haired girl, then another and another. The stocky
boy called out in ecstasy:

" Look."

They came one by one, on tiptoe, with reverence, heard
the awesome news that I was the owner, they fingered it,
the red-head screamed with delight and Julio declared:

" If anybody ever calls you a mouse, just let me know."

I told him that I could take care of myself and somebody
suggested that we should choose the teams again and that
I should be one of the captains who chose. Julio explained
that they had a coin earlier to toss, but having chosen
teams, they spent it. I produced one of my coins, a one
New-Franc coin of shining silver. We tossed, I won and
chose Julio. More children came and stood in the door
against the dusty rays of the glaring sun and were told the
astonishing piece of news about my new football. The
ginger-haired girl said I should call her Julita and if I
wanted to she could show me how I could buy for all of
us jam and bread for one single New-Franc only. I looked
around and found there were fifteen of us and I said it was
impossible, and we raced after her to the end of the Spanish
Street, leaving the poor little crooked ball, humbled and
forgotten, at the bottom of the stairs, with its owner, a
six-year-old called Gusano, who was allowed into the teams
on account of being the owner of the only ball they had.

Now nobody wanted either him or his crooked ball and he just sat there in miserable loneliness, tears coming into his eyes. We forgot him as soon as we turned the corner, led by Julita's red hair like a red flag. She put on the brakes and explained the plan. First we bought a fair-sized fresh bread, not the loafy sort, but a farm-bread which spread in every direction. It cost me one whole New-Franc with the jam still to come. She broke off the top, dug into it and scooped out the soft inside, leaving only the hard crust. Next we went to the grocer on the other side of the street. She spoke fluent French, she pointed at the small barrels containing different sorts of jam and covered with sheets of glass so that no flies could get at them and, still, the customers could see their colour and denomination. She asked if, instead of putting a kilo of the copper-coloured apricot jam into a paper container, it could be poured into her scooped-out bread. The French grocer laughed, weighed the unusual cask and filled it to the brim. She thanked him politely and asked for the price. When the grocer named it, she put on an act of surprise and told the grocer that she had no idea that jam had gone up, she had no idea that it cost so much even before it had gone up. The grocer demanded to know what she was going to do about it and Julita suggested that he take the stuff back as she couldn't pay for it. The grocer fumed, the girl apologised and there was nothing else to do but pour the whole sticky mass back where it came from. We followed her for a distance until she and we gained the freedom of the Spanish Street again. Then we surrounded her holding the hollow crust of bread, now smeared over with a broad layer of jam; Julio opened his enormous pocket-knife and cut up the spoil. It tasted fine. We gulped it down, I inspected everybody's hands and let them wipe

their paws clean before I parted with my new football.
Then I kicked it high. It bounced almost to the height of
the first floor, above the shoemaker's sign. I wanted to
catch it in a spectacular fashion, but what I saw made me
forget the ball, the children, my ambition to be a goalkeeper
—everything. In the window of the flat where Manuel
lived, stood a young man I knew.

First, I couldn't explain to myself how he got there. Slowly
it dawned upon me that he might be Carlos. I asked
Julio.

" Of course," he said, " it's Carlos, the smuggler."

I let them take my football, I even encouraged them to
play without me. I hardly dared to look at the man in the
window. He had pyjamas on and was brushing his jacket.
I knew the cleft in his chin, the wart next to his left eye,
the pimply face, the low forehead, the bushy eyebrows,
I would have known him among a thousand, for I saw him
twice in Viñolas's car while I stood in front of his house
full of dark hatred. They had buried my father, the empti-
ness he left in my heart filled to overflowing with love for
him. And, each time when I thought of his butchers, this
love turned into an immense mountain of loathing, pressing
against my chest from the inside, wanting to find a vent to
whistle out into the open. I remembered all who came,
I remembered the cars, the drivers, the passengers, the
sentries, the dogs, the iron gates, the barbed fence, everybody and everything.

Gusano sauntered out of the house, snivelling slightly,
clutching his rejected football. Presumably he would have
stayed in the doorway till nightfall, nursing his headache,
but for the fact that people were coming down the stairs.

A moment after him came Manuel and Pedro, locked in loud conversation. Pedro saw me first.

" Pablo, *amigo*, you come and get your cake."

Manuel knew nothing of the cake, he was only interested in the new football, the way it behaved, the authority it bestowed upon me. He must have thought me rather rude, for I didn't answer his questions, just trotted beside them as they walked towards Pedro's car just round the corner in the main street.

" Have you lost your tongue?" asked Manuel.

I was hiccuping again. We passed the Spanish grocer, Pedro took out a box of matches, lit a cigarette and, suddenly, there was a tremendous flash in front of my eyes as if a thousand match boxes had gone up in flames. It blinded me for a second. When I could see again, I saw Pedro's grinning face.

" Did I frighten you, *amigo*?" he laughed, " the best cure for hiccups. I lit half a dozen matches, that's all."

Now I realised that it had stopped my hiccups. Still, it wasn't fright that stopped them, for I had been frightened before the matches went up. We rounded the corner and I saw Pedro's car. How could I tell them? I followed them in silence. Pedro unlocked the car and while he fumbled for the cake the silent woman had sent me, Manuel put his hand on my shoulder.

" You look as if you had seen a ghost, Pablo."

I assured him I had.

" A ghost?" he asked, sceptically. " Where?"

" I know Carlos," I said.

" That doesn't make him a ghost."

" I have seen him in Pamplona twice."

" What of it? He goes to Pamplona every week. Sometimes twice."

" I have seen him in Viñolas's car. Once with Viñolas and once with Zapater."

Manuel shook his head.

" I don't believe you, Pablo. Pedro," he called into the car, " Pedro, you hear what Pablo says?" Pedro emerged from the car.

" What?"

" He tells me he has seen Carlos in Pamplona with Viñolas."

" Are you sure, Pablo?"

" Once with Viñolas and once with Zapater."

" Perhaps they caught him and took him into the policia," Manuel said, and a weird fire appeared in his eyes.

" It wasn't the policia. It was at Viñolas's house. He's an informer."

Manuel grabbed my shoulders, not angrily, but it hurt.

" Now, don't you say such things. Perhaps you have made a mistake. It's not easy to see a man in a car."

" I can."

" Nobody can. He is my friend. He's doing a lot of things for me. He's been walking all night to let me know about Pilar."

Pedro spat his cigarette into the gutter. " I, for one, don't like him. He's too eager to make you go."

" He spoke to Pilar late last night," Manuel argued.

" How could he? They don't let people into a hospital late at night," Pedro said.

" He knows a nurse in the ward. He takes her scent from here. And nylon stockings. Girls do anything for scent and stockings. She let him in after midnight. He quoted to me what Pilar said." He paused. " He wouldn't dare to inform on me. He knows I would murder him."

Pedro had to lower his voice as some people were passing the car.

" If you're killed in Pamplona, you can't murder anyone."

Manuel saw the logic in this. Pedro thought they ought to go back to the flat and make Carlos talk. The two of them could surely persuade him to tell the truth. Manuel didn't like to persuade anybody in France. He had had no trouble with the authorities here and did not wish to have any.

I said: " Don't go over, Manuel."

He shook his head, not to me, but to himself. As if he had said something to himself and had disagreed with it. Pedro found the cake and held it, not knowing what to do with it. At last, Manuel spoke.

" We'll go back to the flat and ask him. But no persuasion."

We all trooped back along the Spanish Street. I saw my football at the far end of the lane and heard the children's excited cries. I would have given anything to be with them. And I would have given a lot if I needn't have gone upstairs with Manuel and Pedro. We climbed the stairs in silence, found Carlos dressing and lacing up his shoes. He looked up without much surprise.

" What's up? Forgotten something?"

Manuel pointed to me. " Have you ever seen this boy, Carlos?"

Carlos stared at me, then shook his head.

" Who is he?"

" He says he saw you going to Viñolas's in his car."

Carlos screwed up his eyes. Then he started to grin.

" Me? With Viñolas! Who the hell is this boy?"

Pedro told him and explained to him that I had come over quite recently.

Carlos finished the business with his shoes as if the whole matter were too ridiculous to talk about. Then he looked at me.

" The boy is either mixing me up with another man, or he's just lying."

Pedro put his hand on my shoulder. " Why should Pablo be lying?"

" I don't know. I don't know why boys lie and I don't know why this particular boy tells a lie. I have other things to worry about. And I'm beginning to be sorry about taking all this trouble to bring messages from Pilar. If that's all the thanks I get for it."

Manuel tried to pacify him. " Don't take it wrongly, Carlos. I know how much I owe you."

This started Carlos off enumerating his recent achievements, the toil he had put in to bring news from Pilar, the money he had spent on buying presents for nurses, the time he had wasted in Pamplona getting to Pilar and the dangers all these activities entailed for him.

I said: " Pilar is dead."

They stared at me with surprise. Carlos thought I was out of my mind, Pedro asked how could I know a thing like that. Manuel declared that though she might have been alive during the night when Carlos spoke to her, she might have died since, and if I was psychic I could have a feeling about it.

" She died at eight o'clock last night," I told them.

" Who said so?" asked Manuel.

" The priest."

" What priest?"

I had to tell them about the priest who came from Pamplona to warn Manuel, about the letter and the message he left with me.

" Where is the letter?" Carlos asked.

" I tore it up and threw the pieces into there." I showed them the lavatory. " Perhaps there are a few bits still there. They wouldn't go down. I tried several times." How I wished that those bits would still be in the bowl. Pedro lifted the lid. There was nothing but clean water in the bowl.

" Where did the priest go?" Carlos wanted to know.

" To Lourdes."

" What did he come for?"

" He said Pilar had asked him . . .!"

Carlos burst into a fit of laughter. " That's a good one. Pilar asking a priest. Did you hear that? What else did he say?"

" She asked him to warn Manuel not to go. If she were dead, it was not worth while for Manuel to risk his life."

Carlos shook with laughter. " She said she was dead? That tops the lot." He turned to Manuel. " This boy is the greatest little liar I've come across. Where did you get hold of him?"

Manuel sat down on a chair. He looked tired and I thought he looked very old. He got hold of my arms, grabbing also my lapels, my shirt and my skin. The shirt buttons flew off, it hurt me. What Carlos said hurt me more.

" Look, the little rogue! He's wearing a cross!"

I stammered that it belonged to my mother, but I knew I had lost. How could they ever believe me, having found out that I wore a cross hidden under my shirt. Carlos made an attempt to tear it off but Manuel whirled me around. His voice sounded dead tired.

" If there was a priest, Pablo, why didn't you tell me?"

" I wanted you to go. The children say you are a mouse. I wanted you to show them. . . ."

He let my arm go. He needed both hands to wipe his face. It was not dirty or sweaty, he just wiped it for wiping's sake. Pedro lowered his head and I started to cry. What a silly thing to do, I thought, here I was taking part in men's business and behaving like a baby. I heard Carlos saying to Manuel:

" A priest came to warn you? A *priest*? Since when have priests liked you so much? After what you did to them in that church. Don't you know that the clergy are the best allies of the police in Spain? Do you believe that Pilar asked a priest to take a message to you? The next thing you'll tell me is that *you*, too, are a bosom friend of the priests. Do you believe this bloody little liar rather than me who saw Pilar a few hours ago?"

" Shut up," said Manuel. " If that priest has gone to Lourdes, he can be found there."

Pedro nodded and Manuel stood up. Carlos told them to go alone, he had more important things to do. But Manuel said: " You're coming." And he said to me: " You're coming, too."

Pedro had a gun on him. He kept it close under his armpit in a leather holster, the holster being attached to one of his braces. Before we left the flat, Manuel asked him for it. " You'll be driving, let me have it." Pedro undid the buckle and handed it to him, he opened its lock very expertly, examined it, put it into his right-hand pocket and left his hand with it in the pocket. He never once looked at Carlos, but Carlos was watching his movements closely.

I was worried for many reasons. First, I was worried

about my new football. When we walked along the street,
Julio had run up to us.

"Aren't you coming?" he asked.

I shook my head. He went on:

"Can we go on playing with it?"

I nodded and he ran off, followed by the gang. I hoped
he would take care of it and would give it back to me when
the proper time came and I wasn't a prisoner any longer as
I was now. It occurred to me that, after what had happened,
Manuel might take back his present. I certainly did not
deserve it, looking at things from Manuel's point of view.
The second thought that haunted me was that they had
expected me for lunch at home. Antonio would be very
angry when he arrived back from work and had to wait
lunch for me. Perhaps Monique would take my side,
might even admit that she had given me money to go to
the pictures. They would give me another few minutes,
but when I didn't come, they would start eating. The
thought of it made me hungry. I wondered if I could ask
Manuel to release me from going to Lourdes, but I dis-
carded the idea since I knew for certain that he wouldn't.
After all, I was the only one who could recognise the priest.

This priest was worrying me most of all. Why did he
come to warn Manuel, why did he take the trouble? I had
to agree with Carlos, it seemed most unlikely that a priest
would come all the way from Pamplona to warn Manuel,
the bandit. On the other hand, Carlos had turned out to
be an informer, I had seen him talking to Viñolas with my
own eyes and I had seen him with Zapater too. But priests
were liars, scoundrels, idlers, the dregs of society, vermin
like lice, who lived on the poor, frauds, rogues and swind-
lers. Still, either the priest or Carlos was lying. But which
of them? Carlos, the informer or Father Francisco, the

priest? What I knew of Carlos came from my own knowledge; what I knew about priests originated from other people. But those other people who condemned the clergy included my father, and my father would not have condemned them if they hadn't deserved it. On the other hand, my mother didn't loathe them, she even wanted to be buried by them. But, of course, women were weak and changed their minds often, you couldn't rely on their judgment, they would do anything for scent and nylon stockings, just as Manuel said. But my mother never had scent, or nylon stockings. Neither had Pilar.

I sat next to Pedro in the front, Manuel and Carlos sat in the back. We spoke little. Once Pedro asked which road to take, the one through Gelos or the other which runs along the right bank of the Gave, or a third, along the main road to Tarbes. Manuel did not mind. Carlos gave his own opinion, at this time of day the main road would be the fastest, so Pedro took the main road. I found it strange that Carlos spoke as if everything was in order with him. He seemed to be sure of himself, he wanted to get as quickly as possible to Lourdes to dispose of all these silly doubts about his honour. Or was it just bravado? Bluffing up to the last second. He started to whistle, not really whistling, just blowing air through his pursed lips.

The road to Tarbes was wide and very fast. We passed through a place called Soumoulou and Pedro asked me if I knew where the Rue Soumoulou was in Pau. I told him that it was the real name of the Spanish Street.

Manuel said: " He's got a fine memory, Pablo has."

I saw him in the mirror and I saw Carlos, too. Carlos stopped whistling. Shortly after Soumoulou we branched off on the road N 640. We were now only 23 kilometres from Lourdes, a mere 15 minutes' driving. There were only a few cars on the road. Pedro said all the drivers were at lunch. This made me very hungry. I licked my lips and Pedro asked me if I wanted any of the cake. I offered it to all three but none of them took any. It was a good cake, walnuts and chocolate and a sort of marzipan centre. I wondered when the silent woman had had the time to make it with all those ducks and cows and Pedro to look after. I also wondered whether Monique could make a cake like this, or whether you could buy chocolate cakes in tins and she just had to use the tin-opener to produce a cake. I thought of her and again I had the strong feeling that though I liked cakes very much, I also liked other things, like that scent and the smoothness of her skin and the richness of her hair and the glint in her eyes which made me keep a secret.

"Here we are," announced Pedro, as we drove into Lourdes. The streets were crowded. Pedro said the streets in Lourdes were always crowded on account of pious people being preoccupied with holiness and restraining themselves in worldly pleasures like eating, hoping to please Heaven. On the other hand the innkeepers were praying to the Holy Virgin to bless all pilgrims with gluttony so that they would consume enormous amounts of food and drink. Pedro seemed to know not only the frame of mind of pilgrims and the secret of the innermost successes of innkeepers, but he knew the place itself. He parked the car behind some tiny houses and we walked down to a huge square on the bank of the Gave, called Esplanade des Processions. There were hordes of priests from all sorts of countries. Pedro asked several where he would be most likely to find the Spanish priests and a little fat chap told him that most foreign priests were assembling in the subterranean cathe-

dral, though some of them might still be at the Grotto of
the Holy Virgin, one or two might even be taking the baths
in the holy piscine adjoining the Grotto. I would have
liked to watch the procession of the wheel-chairs a little
longer. Pedro explained that in the chairs were the sick
and disabled who came from all corners of the world to
bathe in the holy pool, hoping to be healed by its miraculous
powers. The wheel-chairs crossed the esplanade in endless
procession, pushed by pious visitors, who hoped to gain
favour with Heaven through serving the sick. These chair-
pushers chanted prayers in monotonous singing, taking
little notice of each other. Manuel urged us on. We
found the subterranean cathedral, Pedro asked again where
the Spanish priests would be and a man with a badge
displaying the Holy Virgin directed us to the inside where
huge burning candles in the dark caverns were surrounded
by even darker shapes of priests, most of them holding
flaming tapers, whispering as in expectation of something
exciting just about to happen. You could hear all languages
and the clear harmony of a children's choir. There was
continuous movement of solitary priests carrying their
dripping, smoking wax-candles, lighting up spots and
leaving others completely in the shadow, moving about, but
the general picture remained one of motionless shadows
and fixed flames. The cave seemed endless, the centre of
it, where all the priests had assembled, had been roped off,
leaving a narrow passage along the walls, through this
passage sightseers like ourselves could pass and go the
round. After wandering about and asking repeatedly, we
saw a large group and we knew that they were Spanish.
There is something in Spanish people's faces and eyes that
can be recognised, whether they are priests or just normal

people. Pedro asked another usher with a holy badge pinned to his lapel if they were from Spain?

" Yes," he said and smiled as if Pedro had said something funny, " those are from Lérida, those there come from the Zaragoza district, those from Pamplona and those, on the far side, from Barcelona. Are you looking for someone?"

We left him standing and wormed our way closer to the Pamplona lot.

" Can you see him?" asked Carlos.

But I couldn't. I went as close as the rope would let me, looked into their faces, but none of them was Father Francisco.

" Let's go," said Manuel and for the first time he took his hand out of his right-hand pocket. He moved towards the exit, leaving Carlos to follow him. Pedro asked the usher:

" Are they all here? Or are any of them missing?"

Holy badge nodded. " One is at the holy pool. Here he comes."

We saw a smiling man in his black robe approaching. As he came close to Manuel and Carlos he stopped, staring at them, the smile died on his face, his lips began to twitch, tears started to run down his cheeks. Manuel passed him without noticing and Pedro grabbed my arm.

" Is that the one?"

I shook my head. We went out into the dazzling sunlight. Women from a strange land were crossing the centre of the esplanade, unhurriedly, aimlessly, with scarves over their heads, in heavy boots and coloured stockings. Manuel stopped and said to me:

" You have been lying, you bloody brat." At the same moment he slapped my face with such force that I thought he must have bashed in my head. It hurt and burnt and

I felt a terrible hatred for him and wished that he should
be caught by Viñolas and beaten to a cripple, and I started
to hiccup and spat out a tooth. Pedro pulled me away
from him because I went for him in a blind rage. Carlos
said that I deserved far more punishment than just slapping
my face and I tried to kick him and he caught my foot and

I fell on my back, but I could not feel any pain, my fury
had deadened all my senses. He said he had no intention
of staying with us for a moment longer and Manuel could
go to hell and so could Pedro. He left us standing and
disappeared into the crowd which gathered around us,
commenting unfavourably on the performance we had been
putting up in the holy city of Lourdes.

We came to the car. Manuel took the front seat next to
Pedro, letting me climb into the rear.

" Back to Pau? " asked Pedro, and Manuel nodded.

" I want to stop at The Place. I'll need the Thompson."

So we took the road on the right bank of the Gave.

I felt miserable, full of hatred and without a single friend. Not before we reached St. Pé did either of them speak.

" Are we going to-night?" asked Pedro.

" I suppose so," came from Manuel. He didn't sound very enthusiastic.

We passed through St. Pé and were nearing Bétharram when I spotted him. He was walking towards us, covered with dust, you could hardly see the black of his cassock.

" There he is," I called.

The car passed him, the brakes screeched, Manuel shouted and Pedro backed up the car.

" That's him. That's Father Francisco."

Manuel told him to get into the car, he did so without asking a word, falling on to the seat beside me like a log.

" Oh, you are the boy," he said, and when he heard Manuel telling Pedro to drive on, he leaned forward to have a good look at him. " You must be Artiguez. So you got my message."

Manuel asked: " What the hell are you doing here, walking?"

Father Francisco sighed. " I had no money and Father Erasmus has got my railway ticket."

Pedro turned, forgetting his driving for a moment. " You mean you've been walking all the way from Pau?"

" Not all the way. I got a lift soon after I left Pau. But the car had to branch off to a place called Bénéjacq. Later I got another lift almost as far as Bétharram. I've done quite well really." He looked through the window, anxiously. " Where are you taking me?"

" Back to Pau," said Manuel.

The priest got very agitated. " You can't do that. I have to join up with my group at Lourdes."

" No one is missing you there."

"But I have come to Lourdes. . . ."

"You are going to Pau, Priest," said Manuel. "Don't get excited, keep quiet and you will come to no harm." The priest sighed again and remained silent. Manuel went on: "What is this about coming to tell me not to go to Pamplona?" The priest wanted to answer, but Manuel hadn't finished. "No lies now, Priest, or you will get into such trouble that your hell would seem heaven to you."

He stopped and waited. The priest waited, too. I watched them. Here I was, witnessing the great man in action. But his foe was just a paltry priest, a miserable clergyman whom a child could have outwitted and two children could have beaten up. *And,* to add insult to injury, he seemed quite brave. Not a bit of panic. Manuel spoke again.

"You told Pablo that my mother had spoken to you."

"Yes," agreed the priest.

"You are lying. Pilar wouldn't speak to a priest."

We were passing two policemen on bicycles. They were smoking and talking seriously, probably of women as The Flute told me the day I crossed the Verderiz. Father Francisco saw them, too. He did not answer Manuel's sneer and Manuel got more and more angry with him since the priest maintained that Pilar had sent for him just before she died, having guessed that the police had set a trap for Manuel and seeking the priest's help to warn him. Manuel didn't believe a word.

"You know me, Priest? You know what I did to those priests in the church?"

Father Francisco nodded. Manuel told me to move to the right, he climbed over the front seat to sit in the back so that the priest sat between the two of us now. Manuel grabbed his arm and forced him to turn.

" You want me to believe that a man in your garb would risk his life to warn me? Or aren't you a priest?" He shook the young man by the shoulder and, suddenly, slapped his face. " Answer me. You're one of Viñolas's informers, aren't you?"

I hated Manuel for this almost as much as I loathed him when he slapped my own face. I saw tears appear in the priest's eyes. I had never seen a grown-up man crying and I never wish to see another. At other times I would have despised a man for bursting into tears, but now I detested only the man who caused it.

" I'm going to confront you with Carlos," announced Manuel. " One of you is lying."

I said: " Carlos is lying," and Manuel reminded me that nobody had asked me. That was true, but there was no need to remind me of it. Especially as he knew now that I had been telling the truth and that he had slapped me without the slightest justification. He shook the priest once more.

" You know Carlos, don't you?"

Father Francisco remembered the name, and the man, and asked if Carlos had been in Pamplona last night. When told that he had, he said that he saw Carlos in the company of Viñolas and heard him saying that Manuel wouldn't be coming yesterday.

" What time yesterday?" asked Manuel and took his hand off the priest.

" Shortly after eight last night."

" Impossible. He left Pau only after nine in the morning."

Now Pedro chimed in: " Could be. If he works with

the police, they would pick him up and take him by car to Pamplona."

This made sense and Manuel let it pass. He said: " Still, you'll never make me believe that this priest has risked his life to travel to Pau to warn me." He paused and then he added: " I'll see what Carlos has to say to that."

I was wondering how he would find out since Carlos wasn't here and probably would never come back. Pedro must have had the same thought.

" You'll never see *him* again."

Manuel disagreed. " He doesn't know that we have picked up the priest. He'll come back to-night."

Father Francisco wondered: " You want to keep me till to-night?"

" I shall keep you as long as I like. Until I have found out what I want to know."

The priest shook his head in despair. " Our train is going back in the morning."

" Shut up!" said Manuel, and we were wrapped in silence until we reached the outskirts of Pau. Pedro nodded at a signpost.

" Jurançon. They make a good wine here."

" You can have it," was all Manuel's reaction.

Pedro turned back, hurt. " What's wrong with it?"

" You watch the road," said Manuel and I could see that Pedro didn't like being spoken to like that.

It was almost three o'clock when we dropped Manuel and Father Francisco at the corner of the Spanish Street. Pedro was to go back to his silent woman and Manuel promised to let him know during the night what happened. I, too, got out to have a look at what the children were up to and, most important, what had become of my new football.

The street seemed pretty empty. No children were about and I thought "Good-bye, new football!" I didn't care much. Though Manuel slapped my face unjustly, it was more likely than not, that he would take it back. He still had a foul temper and, since I didn't care for him any more, he was welcome to take it back. There were other footballs in this world, though none of them felt and bounced better than mine. I could be an expert goalkeeper with the crooked ball belonging to Gusano just as well. More so —there was more to it to be a crack shot with a rusty old gun than with a brand-new, well-oiled automatic.

Just before they left me, Manuel spoke to me.

"Are you going home, Pablo?"

I did not feel like talking to him, but his foul temper seemed to have left him, he sounded rather sad and I said yes.

"I'm sorry to have slapped you," he went on. He waited for me to say something, but what can you say when somebody tells you that he is sorry for slapping your face. "Are you still cross?" he asked. I shook my head and wished he would leave me alone. But he wouldn't go. "I want to see you before I go. *If* I have to go." I said nothing as I couldn't think of anything to say. He took it the wrong way. "You don't believe I shall go, do you?"

"There is no reason to go now," I said.

"That depends on what I find out from Carlos. *And* this priest." He looked at the priest, the priest looked right back. Suddenly Manuel flared up: "You bloody lot, you all want me to go."

He turned and escorted the priest away.

Pedro sighed. I sat down beside him. He sighed again. Then he let in the clutch.

He dropped me at the corner in front of the bistro,

Le Navarre, saying he must be getting on. He told me also that he did not care to see Antonio. They didn't get on well, he said, Antonio having turned out, against his expectations, a traitor to the Spanish cause, to whom it did not matter whether monarchists, Fascists, or The People governed the country, as long as he himself earned enough to fill his belly. Antonio took a foreign wife, and that showed what sort of character he turned out to be. I wanted to ask what was wrong with foreign wives, if they had nice soft hair and smelt so good. He must have anticipated it, for he added:

" I hear she carries on. . . ." He stopped and I didn't know what he meant. I certainly had never seen Monique carrying anything much.

He remembered the cake, shook hands with me and told me not to take too much to heart the things Manuel said, and especially the smack. I watched his car reach the main road and disappear. I felt very lonely. How well this day had started and how awful it had turned out later. Grown-ups had a way of messing things up. I hated to go home, for I knew that there would be trouble. Sure enough, the waiter recognised me and told me that my uncle and aunt were looking for me, asking the neighbours if they had seen me. The waiter was rubbing his bloodshot eye and I remembered him rubbing it before when I arrived with Marcel the first time, and it occurred to me that on that day I couldn't understand a single word of French and now, only ten days later, I had a vague notion what this French jabber meant, so I was getting on much better than Antonio would admit. Antonio always used this learning of French to discourage me from going to the Spanish Street. Well, he'd be happy to hear that I wouldn't go there any more. I wouldn't, for I did not wish to hear the children teasing me

about Manuel, the mighty mouse. Not having a new
football any more, they would call me a mouse, too, and
Julio would certainly withdraw his protection which he
had promised this morning.

I took a long time to walk up the stairs and to ring the
bell. Monique opened the door. She shouted: "*Voilà*
Pablo," and put her arms around me. And Antonio came
and he wasn't angry at all, he smiled and said that they were
very worried having heard that I had left the Spanish Street
with the old bandit, Manuel Artiguez, and two other men,
and they thought I had been kidnapped. They planned to
wait till six o'clock and if I hadn't turned up by then, they
were going to the police. The trouble about me started
when, at noon, a Spanish boy, called Julio, came to the
furniture factory where he knew Antonio worked, and
brought a football, asking Antonio to give it to me as the
boys had to go home for lunch. Antonio heard from him
that I had left with Manuel, the smuggler, Carlos, and a
third man and I had not come back. This, the children
could not explain, since no one would leave his brand-new
football unattended, unless he had to. Antonio came home
at once to ask Monique if I had arrived here.

At this, Monique said: "You missed that 'monsieur'
who brought you from St. Etienne, what's-his-name? He
came to visit you."

I wanted to ask what she meant, since I knew well that
"monsieur" had come to taste a new wine with Monique
and I couldn't understand either how she had forgotten
that his name was Marcel, but I caught her eye and said
nothing. Instead, she got very busy and asked whether
I wanted some coffee, if I was hungry, and I told her I was
and gave her the cake. I mentioned that the third man with
us was Pedro who had brought me this cake from his wife

E

and they thought it was a very good cake. I said nothing about the priest, or about going to Lourdes, or about my face having been slapped, or about Carlos being a traitor, for I knew Antonio wouldn't understand any of these things, and anyway, I felt I was still under an obligation not to tell about the secrets I shared with Manuel and Pedro.

In the far corner of the corridor, next to the lavatory door, I found my football. Antonio wanted to know how I got it and when I told him that Manuel had given it to me, he asked: "What for?" I said, perhaps because he knew my father, and Antonio thought that might well be the reason. He didn't like me having presents from Manuel, he would rather buy me a football himself if I had to have one. I told him, I liked this one and Monique took my side and said it wasn't polite to turn down a present and I thought, perhaps that was the reason why she hadn't turned down the bottles of wine Marcel brought her and she did not mention about it to Antonio because he did not know that it was discourteous to turn down a present.

She prepared a meal for me in no time. While I was gulping it down, Antonio said it wasn't too late to take out the car and go for a drive. She agreed and suggested that we go to Lourdes which I certainly would be interested to see, and told me that in Lourdes there was a Grotto and people in wheel-chairs who hoped to be cured after taking a bath in the holy piscine, and there was a subterranean cathedral, and Antonio thought it an excellent idea.

I thought of Father Francisco who wanted so much to go to Lourdes that he had walked almost the whole way to get there, and who had been taken a prisoner by Manuel Artiguez, the bandit. And here I was, being taken to Lourdes by car twice on the same day.

6

THE WAGES OF SIN is death. I have sinned, now I am earning the wages of my sin. I could have run but I was tired. Perhaps I would not run even if I weren't. My black robe never felt heavier than now, little puffs of dust rose from it when we passed open doorways and a cool breeze hit us. The man beside me walked in silence. He didn't even look at me. I wondered what he would do if I tried to run away. If I dashed into one of these doorways, bolted up the stairs, hammered at a door and called for help? He walked along the wall, on the inside of the pavement, possibly to prevent just that. Marching on the outside gave me a feeling of freedom, though it had no practical significance at all. This morning the street seemed teeming with people, now it was empty. No children were playing about, no shoppers, no strollers, and no shops open. I could see no one in the windows, our steps echoed loud and lonely in the silent, frozen heat of the afternoon. The entire length of the street was in shade now. This morning a thousand shapes of sunlight streaked the walls, now monotonous sombre colours prevailed. This morning everything had appeared to glitter, I had the satisfaction of mending what I had done wrong the day before. Even the long walk to Lourdes seemed to lighten by burden, my aching feet cheered me up. When that woman stopped her car and offered me a lift, I shook my head, thanked her and walked on. She spoke no Spanish, she kept on talking to me, driving very slowly alongside, trying to persuade me to change my mind and finally, getting fed up, accelerated, letting the engine roar, she waved and left me behind in a cloud of dust. Later, of course, I did accept a lift, but I did it because it was getting late and I wanted to get to Lourdes as soon as possible. It was a young man this time who spoke a little Spanish and worked at his father's farm near Bétharram. He had gone to Pau to fetch spare parts for a tractor, broken the previous day. He had forgotten to note the number of the broken parts and now worried in case he had brought the wrong sizes. Meeting me cheered him up, for meeting a priest was lucky and he was sure that the spares would prove to be right.

" In here," said Manuel Artiguez. We climbed the stairs, I first, he following, like a warden follows a prisoner. I heard him breathing in a measured way, taking the steps sparingly and cautiously as a mountaineer climbs a rock face. He must have climbed many wild passes to elude the frontier guards of two countries. He opened the door and bid me enter. " Now," he said, " there is nothing else but to wait. He might come soon or he might come late. But he'll come for sure and then we'll see who is lying."

We entered a bare room with a door to another room.

He looked into that second room but found nothing there
and closed the door again. I asked him if I could sit down?
He nodded. On the chair near the window was a rucksack.
This reminded him of something. He went next door and
came back with another rucksack. They were different in
size and were differently packed. The one he fetched was
much larger, packed higgledy-piggledy and contained
besides a shaving-kit, various flat boxes. He tore open the
thin layer of transparent film and opened one of the boxes.
There were several pairs of women's stockings in it. He
pulled them from the box, let them dangle in front of me.
" You know what these are, Priest?"

I told him they were stockings.

" Have you ever seen them on a woman's legs?"

Of course I had seen them. Women wear them in the
cities. Perhaps not such fine ones, but almost. He sneered:
" You know what I mean, Priest. I mean have you seen
them on a young woman's legs, right up. Right up to here?
Under her skirt. Here, where the clasps hold them tight?
One here, another on the opposite side. Two clasps with
two bands of elastic, running up to her belt. And between
the belt and this stocking there is cool firm flesh. For
some reason, the flesh there is always cool."

I let him talk. All at once, he forgot to tease me. He
began to wonder why Carlos had brought back nylon
stockings from Spain. They were French nylons and he
knew that Carlos took dozens of pairs every week to
Spain. They were, in fact, Carlos's main merchandise.
Why did he bring them back to France? Even if he had
hurried back to tell the news about Pilar, he could have left
them with someone. It was foolish to cart them all the
way back to France. He opened more boxes, pulled out
more stockings. There were different shades and some

seemed thinner than the others. Then he tried to fold them as they were before, but he couldn't. He lost his temper and stuffed them back into the rucksack, boxes and their contents in a frightful mess. He flung down the lot and turned to me.

" Do you worship Jesus Christ?"

" Yes."

" Why doesn't He help you now?"

I said that the Lord might be doing just that. Often we are not aware of it, but later we realise His purpose. " Take my own case with your mother. She heard the matron talking to my substitute about my going to Lourdes. God made her overhear their conversation. She knew that I was the only living person who would have a chance to warn you, for the police had set a trap to kill you. Now, how could she ask me to help her? The Lord gave her an idea: To say that she wanted to receive the sacrament, and from nobody else but me."

He listened incredulously, and I went on:

" Observe how clear His way is and still, how obscure to us. She offered me a deal. She said: You warn my son and I will take your sacrament. The Lord knew that I was not humble enough, He knew that I would turn down her suggestion. But He knew also that I should repent when I had heard that she had died and redouble my efforts to warn you. I tried to make it easy for myself. I wrote you a letter, I thought it would be enough. But when I got out of the train, He made me miss that train. And also, how do you explain finding me on the road? There are many roads I could have taken. Twice I had accepted lifts. I could have been sitting in a car when you passed me."

He stared at me. It took him some time to voice his

doubt. " Why wasn't I here when you came this morning? Why did you only find the boy in the flat? And why didn't He let you get to Lourdes?"

" I don't know. Perhaps he didn't wish me to go to Lourdes. Perhaps He wanted *you* to go there. Perhaps He had a purpose in your going to Lourdes."

" What purpose could that be?"

" Who knows? One day we might find out. We might be mere tools, instrumental in something that doesn't even concern us."

He stared again. He took Carlos's rucksack back to the other room, came in and asked if I would like some coffee? He made it there on the table, explaining that there wasn't any kitchen in the flat. It tasted fine. I hadn't eaten all day. The same thing must have occurred to him for he brought a big sausage out from a drawer, a knife and two plates. He cut a thick slice for me and cut one for himself.

" I haven't got anything but water," he said. He went to the bathroom and fetched water in a jug. When he left me, unattended, he looked back from the door. It was the last flicker of suspicion he showed towards me.

Time passed slowly, with long periods of silence, and fits of talking. He never agreed with what I said, but sometimes he did not disagree. One thing he just couldn't stomach at all: he couldn't understand why I had come to warn him.

" If Carlos is an informer and I stay put and Viñolas finds out that someone has warned me, it'll be easy for him to guess who gave the game away. He will arrest you. Aren't you scared?"

" A little. No, it is not true. I'm scared. I should hate to be locked up with criminals. And I abhor violence."

" Not all the inmates of Spanish prisons are criminals."
He paused. " Even those whom *you* would call *criminals*
aren't." Once more he waited for some reaction from me.
" You would call *me* a criminal. Do you think I raided all
those places in Spain for money? How much do you
think we got from the post office in Pamplona? A few
thousand pesetas, that's all. And a hundred thousand
stamps. My gang and I want to show the people that those
at the top are not almighty. We want Spaniards to know
that those who kick them have not yet forgotten wincing.
We want every henchman of Viñolas to remember that the
day will come when he'll be tortured for torturing others.
Now the young generation is different. A smuggler
smuggles for his own benefit. A thief breaks into places
to steal. I raid to destroy. I have destroyed a million's worth
of property, but this is how I live." He spread his arms.
" Even this lousy flat I share with Carlos. I kept a little
money, true. I have to live."

So he went on and I listened. From time to time he got
up and walked from one end of the room to the other and
back. Just like a caged animal, forgetting that I was in
his cage. But the slightest movement, a sound from the
street, a whiff from the window, or a sigh from me, could
arouse violence in him. I pulled my chair closer to the table
and table and chair propped up my tired body between
them. It reminded me of the train this morning when I sat
at the window, with a small table between me and Father
Esteban, watching dawn break upon the landscape. This
morning my thoughts were centred round this man who
now sat opposite me. And now, I thought of the train, and
its gentle swaying. I felt its swinging and throbbing, but
knew that it was my head bobbing from exhaustion. I
heard the whistle of the train, the clatter of running through

stations, the pulsation of sorting out its proper path among the rails. It seemed that I was travelling back to Pamplona. The train halted with a jerk, a man in uniform stepped into the compartment and touched my arm. " Wake up, Priest. Priest, do you hear me?"

I woke up with Manuel, the bandit, hovering over me.

" Wake up, Priest."

I mumbled something. It was dark. Manuel said: "He won't come back to-night. I'll switch on the light."

When he did, there was laughter outside on the landing, and then the sound of feet rushing down the stairs. Manuel ran to the door and opened it wide. From far below, the man burst into another roar of laughter as he scurried into the street. Manuel screamed after him: "Carlos," he roared, " Carlos, come back!" He well knew that Carlos wouldn't come back and that he had no chance of catching him. He hurried to the window of the other room, switching off the light in ours. He leaned out of the window and fired two shots after Carlos, but the sound of running feet did not falter. He came away from the window, lit up faintly by the light from the street, cursing and putting away his gun. I could see that one or two lights went on in the houses opposite, excited people were calling to each other, asking questions in Spanish. Manuel said: " I missed him. He must have been standing on the landing all the time, listening to find out whether I was inside."

I asked him why he thought that the man was Carlos? He said it couldn't be anybody else. Carlos had come back for his rucksack, for the nylon stockings. He had little else to come back for. Now he'll never come back. He will cross into Spain and move to the south, since no traitor could live in the north. He would tell Viñolas that his mouse-trap wouldn't work, the mouse had been tipped-off about the trap.

Manuel stood in the door of the next room, listening to the sounds in the street. People were discussing where the shots had come from. One said they were not shots at all: a gust of wind had banged a shutter, or a door, or a window. A voice argued that a man was heard running down the street, another had heard him laughing. It was more likely that the running man had fired the shots. No man who is a target would scream with laughter. If it were a shot, it came from the running man. The fruity voice of a woman reasoned that neither the man who fires a gun, nor a person the shots were intended for, would be amused. The spots of light on the wall of the other room went out one by one, the voices ceased gradually. Manuel came back to the table.

" You've been asleep a long time."

I asked him what the time was.

" After midnight. When is that train of yours due?"

" Leaves Lourdes at nine in the morning."

He figured out when it would be in Pau. Then, suddenly, he said: " I wouldn't take that train if I were you." He seemed genuinely concerned. " You'll be arrested. I can't do anything about Carlos. If I knew where he would cross, I'd go after him. But I don't. He can take a dozen different passes. I could go after him and catch him in Pamplona. Perhaps I will."

I pleaded with him not to go. " If you do go, all that I've done will have been in vain. Leave it to me, I won't be put into prison so easily. The clergy can take care of themselves." He acknowledged this with a sneer. " Do you think, Priest, I want to go in order to save *you*? If I go, I go to kill Carlos."

"Must you kill somebody?" I asked. "Why do you always want to kill? Let him be. If he is to be punished, he will be."

"By whom?"

I shrugged, but he couldn't see this in the dark, so he answered his question himself. "You priests sermonise that God likes us to lend a hand occasionally. He could help the poor, Himself, but He likes us, mortals, to do it. Perhaps He would like me to help Him punish a sinner." He chuckled. "It's funny. It's really funny. Here we are, the three of us: I, Carlos and a priest. Carlos has got away. I'll get away, too, without being caught, I can just stay here sitting on my arse, here in Pau. I might buy a little house near Pedro and be happy ever after. The priest, alone, will suffer. There's no justice for you. How do you explain that, Padre?"

I got angry with him for the first time since I had met him, though I said nothing more than that I was sorry for him. He banged his fist on the table.

"Nobody need be sorry for Manuel Artiguez. There's nothing to be sorry for." He grabbed my arms from across the table and shook me. "What the hell are you sorry for? Come on. Tell me."

I said: "I'm sorry for a man who has nothing but hatred in him."

He took this as the greatest insult. "How do you know, Priest? Because I loathe parsons? I love plenty of people, don't you worry. I love Pedro, I love that boy, Pablo, I loved Pilar."

"You loved your mother and yet you have not mentioned her name since you met me. You jabbered about Viñolas and Carlos and Pedro, you told me at length *why* you kill and why you destroy, and how much you plundered from the post office."

He hit me hard across the face but I didn't care. I didn't stop either. "You have never asked me what your mother looked like on her death-bed, whether she suffered or passed away in peace. You don't care what her last words were. . . ."

He let my arms go and sat down. He panted in the dark.

"I'll kill you for this," he said, but never was a threat uttered more miserably, or sounded less menacing.

"The only thing you know is killing. I came here as your friend. I did something for you, for which you say I shall be punished. And still you want to kill me. Well, go ahead. Do something, for Heaven's sake. Don't only boast. Don't threaten all the time."

He said nothing. He got up and went to the toilet. I heard it flushing. I rose, tried the door to the stairs, and found it open. He came back.

"You can go if you want to. You can go to hell."

"All right," I said.

"You can wait here if you care. I won't harm you."

I don't quite know why I stayed. Perhaps because he sounded so sad, so utterly hopeless. If he didn't mind, I could just as well stay here till morning. He made coffee in the dark without opening his mouth. Only when he sat down and pushed the jug over to me, he asked:

"Was Pilar . . . was she cross with me?"

"Cross for what?"

"For not coming in time."

"Would she be cross, if her only thought was to save your life?"

"You know why I didn't go before?"

"Why should you have gone before? There was no reason?"

"I knew that she was very ill days before. You want to hear why I didn't go?"

I knew he was going to tell me whether I wished to hear it or not. So I said: "Why?"

"Because I'm a coward."

"You, a coward?"

"Everybody in Pau knows it. The children write it on the walls. You see, since that bullet was taken out of my neck, I can't move so freely as all that. The neck is not too bad, but the chest, the legs, the arms get heavy as lead. I just don't know how I could climb over the pass. I don't know whether my hands are steady enough to hold a gun. I don't mean to hold it, but to hold it as a gun should be held. You know what I mean? And my nerves . . . They are worse. What can a man do without nerves? I have done enough for one man, don't you think? No man has a higher price on his head in Spain than I have. That proves how much I have done, doesn't it?"

I did not answer. He took it as contradiction.

"You don't believe I have, do you?"

"I do," I said. "You have done enough."

"You want to lie down? There is another bed."

I told him I couldn't sleep now. I wanted to think about to-morrow. What I should say if Viñolas had found out about me. What I should answer if they asked me questions at the seminary. And what I should tell Father Erasmus to-morrow morning. He would be furious and curious to know what had happened to me.

He tried his best to help.

"Listen, it will be your word against Carlos's. He will tell Viñolas that you came to warn me. Why don't you just say that Carlos is lying?" He pondered about this. "No. It's no good. The facts are against you. You were one of the few who knew about the trap. You had spoken to Pilar. You had travelled to Pau. . . . Tell me, would your fellow-priests lie to save you?"

"They wouldn't. And I wouldn't let them."

"It's nonsense, Priest. If they declared that you had never left them . . . you travelled with them to Lourdes, arrived there Saturday morning, visited the Grotto, went with them to all the places, slept at the Spanish dormitory . . . I suppose there *is* a Spanish dormitory in Lourdes?"

There was. But I would rather tell the truth. And so would the others. He flared up. "Listen, it's suicide. *I* would do anything to save a friend. Surely your fellow-priests would do a little thing like that for you?"

"It's not like that," I tried to explain. "Moreover, I have got a good case."

"Let me hear it. I'm Viñolas, you're yourself. I have arrested you for helping Manuel Artiguez, the bandit, to escape the trap the police had laid for him. How can you explain that? What is your defence?"

"I am a priest. A dying woman has implored me to give a message to her son. I have done nothing more than that."

"But her son was a bandit on the run. A brigand, an enemy of the State, on whose head there is a price."

"For a priest there should be no brigands and no bandits. There is no hatred, only love. No lies, only truth. No police-prisoners, only fugitives. No enemies, only friends."

He sighed. "Words, words. Priest, words won't save you."

He rose and told me that he would lie down for an hour

or so and I had better do the same. I didn't have to take off anything. Just shoes. It would be better for my feet, after all that walking. He locked the hall door, but left the key in the lock. He went to the next room, leaving the door ajar. I heard him stretching his heavy frame on a moaning bed. I undid my shoes and sat at the table, leaning on folded arms. His bed creaked. You could tell, as he spoke, that he had sat up.

" You're very wrong if you think I don't care for my friends. I would do anything for Pedro. Did you know that I bought a football for the boy? Did you?"

I told him I didn't.

" Well, I did. Although I had only met him yesterday. So don't tell me I'm a bad friend."

The bed sighed as he fell back on it. But in no time he sat up again. "And don't tell me that I'm an ungrateful son either. I worked side by side with Pilar when I was six. My father never stayed at home. He carted firewood to Puente la Reina all day, loading the donkeys at dawn, never coming back before nightfall."

I said: "Where was that?"

" Guirguillano. Half-way between Puente la Reina and the Swamps of Alloz. You've heard of the Pantano de Alloz?"

" I was born in Lorca."

The bed creaked again, a second later he appeared in the door, shoeless, and holding up his unbuttoned trousers with both hands.

" Not Lorca on the main road to Estella?"

" The same."

" Impossible."

" I used to be a choir-boy in San Pedro de la Rúa in Estella."

" San Pedro de la Rúa," he repeated. " Would you believe it? So we are neighbours. You know, I never think of priests being born at all."

He stood in the dimness of the door, surprised and enchanted. " Fancy that. When did you go to Pamplona?"

" In thirty-eight."

" Your father had a job there?"

" My father was killed in the civil war. My mother died two years later."

" Which side did he fight for?"

" He fought for no side."

" How's that?"

" One night a band of soldiers came. It was late. They heard of our two donkeys and they came to requisition them. My father refused to give them up. The donkeys were our livelihood. The soldiers threatened him with their guns, my father grabbed one of their rifles and was shot. They took the donkeys and left his body in the yard. We never found out who the soldiers were, which army they belonged to, the fight was then what they called ' fluid ', skirmishing parties penetrated each other's positions, one day we had one side in the village, the next day the other. I was only eight. People came wanting to help, everybody asking, as you are asking, which side my mother belonged to? My mother said: ' I'm on no side, I'm against both sides.' And when they argued that she must make up her mind which side she wanted to ask for help for herself and her child, she said: ' I don't want any help and as for my son, I have chosen a third side for him, the side of the Lord.' The people went, convinced that she had lost her reason because of what had happened to her husband, but she sent me with an old woman to

Pamplona, to the seminary, and wrote to the bishop asking him to make a priest out of me."

"Well," Manuel said, "and you are from Lorca. Would you believe it? Both of us from the same district. Only a few kilometres away. Both had donkeys to grow up with. Both lost our fathers when very young. And you became a priest and I . . . Would you believe it? What's your name?"

"Francisco."

"Francisco? Would you believe it? Mind you, those soldiers were Fascists. They sound Fascists to me. We wouldn't take the donkeys from a poor family. Or certainly not without a chit. Did you get a chit? No? Well, just as I say, they were Fascists. Did you ever go back to Lorca?"

He came to the table to join me. Then he got up and brought over his own rucksack, while I told him that I had returned to Lorca once to visit my mother's grave.

"Did you? Well, your mother had nothing from that. If you visit your mother while she is alive, that's for her. If you visit her grave, that's just for yourself." He undid the rucksack and pulled out a bottle, grinning. "I have got some wine, it wasn't true that I hadn't. But I was keeping it for the trip. Now I suppose I won't be needing it." He fetched two small glasses. "Can you drink wine so late at night?"

"Isn't it rather early morning?" Behind him, in the other room, the pale light of dawn had started to take over from the night. "Yes, I'll be glad to have a glass with you."

He poured out the yellow wine, smiling. "I shouldn't ask a Lorca man a question like that. Well, here's to your safe return."

We drank, it tasted strong and a little acid and transformed one's throat from just an organ to swallow into an important channel of communication between the inside and the outside world, and the news that flowed down was good and exciting. He spoke of wine as the only real elixir of youth.

" It doesn't give you lasting youth, don't get me wrong, but it makes an old man young for an hour or so."

Then, once more, he began to worry about me. What could one do to save me? Why was I so stubborn about not wanting to lie to Viñolas? If only I would—if only the other priests would—everything could turn out right. Even Viñolas would sooner believe a priest than an informer. He argued that, surely, it was one thing to lie to God, and another to lie to the devil. When lying to that devil-incarnate, Viñolas, the sin of lying must be insignificant. If, when asked, I would tell nothing but the truth, nothing could save me.

We finished the bottle, I slept another hour or so and woke up to the noise of the kettle steaming. Manuel was preparing breakfast, laying the table with chipped cups, putting the mighty sausage on a plate. He told me that I had plenty of time and could use his own shaving-kit in the bathroom. I shaved and washed and had boiling hot coffee and plenty of bread with the sausage and he asked what sort of breakfast priests had in the seminary. And if we fasted much and did we have hard beds to sleep on? He said he would come with me to the station and we set off shortly before eight-thirty.

It was Sunday, and the Spanish Street was empty. The bells tolled, the sun was shining. The milkman, with his hand-cart, two cats, Manuel and I were the only souls moving. A woman in a night-shirt opened the shutters in a

flat above the grocer's shop, registered the unusual sight
of Manuel Artiguez accompanying a priest down the lane
with some astonishment, and withdrew instantly. At the
corner Manuel hailed a cab.

" *La gare*," he said, " means station in French."

I asked if he spoke French.

" Just a little. I can't be sold in French."

The cab had to make a detour. I was wondering about
many things. Would the others be on the train? What
am I going to tell them? How are they going to take my
disappearance? And what will happen in Spain? Will
they arrest me as soon as I cross the border?

As if guessing my thoughts, Manuel touched my arm:
" Don't worry, I'll think up something. I'll try to find out
whether Carlos did cross last night."

I thanked him. Of course the danger for me lay not
only in Carlos denouncing me. Even if he chose never to
see Viñolas again, the chief of the policia would figure it
out that I had something to do with it.

The cab stopped, we had arrived. A porter opened the
door and went away disgusted since I was a priest and
priests carry their luggage themselves. He would have
been even more disgusted if he had known that this priest
had no luggage at all.

Manuel said he would wait outside until the train came
in, in case the others were not on it. I had never thought
of that. He held out his hand, I wished him luck and he
said: " I'm glad to have met a Lorca man."

I did not look back, but felt that he was watching me till
I stepped into the building. At the barrier they refused to
let me through without a ticket. There was quite an
argument in French about it. Then a porter appeared who
told a long story to the ticket collector and I recognised

him as one of the people who had witnessed my missing the
train yesterday morning. Finally I got through and stood
on the platform. Quite a number of people were waiting
for the train. I walked to the newspaper kiosk to read the
headlines of the papers, when I discovered two policemen
getting interested in me. I avoided their eyes, but they
came over, one of them consulted a typewritten sheet in
his note-book and spoke: " Father Francisco Roja?"

I nodded.

" Pamplona?"

I nodded again. They found a man who spoke a little
Spanish and told me that it was reported in Lourdes that
one of the Spanish pilgrims had got lost, having missed his
train here, in Pau. I explained how it happened, that I had
spent the day here and was just about to join up with my
party. They nodded gravely, no doubt being glad not to
have to look for me any more. I saw Manuel, in the
distance, watching anxiously what the outcome of my
encounter with the French police would be.

The two policemen stayed with me until the train drew
up beside us. Long before it came to a halt, I saw my
friends crowded in the corridor windows, looking for me,
waving, shouting welcoming words. One of the two policemen shook my hand and both looked as if it had been due to
their own labours that I had been traced and brought back
to the fold. Father Erasmus acknowledged their efforts
with many thanks, uttered in his stilted French. The
conductor urged me to hurry. As soon as I had set my
foot on the carriage step, the train began to move. I looked
back but could not see Manuel. The next moment the
conductor pulled me inside and slammed the door. Father
Erasmus was first to put his arms around me. They let
him come forward, as he was the authority among them.

He seemed genuinely glad to have me back and reproached himself for not letting me have my own ticket and so making it impossible for me to follow them to Lourdes. He wanted to make a strong recommendation to future pilgrims to carry their tickets individually and so be ready to deal with such a predicament as I had found myself in. I was grateful to him for saying this, for it relieved me from going into details of what I had been doing in the twenty-four hours I had spent on my own. They led me triumphantly into the reserved compartment and only when I entered it did I realise that Father Esteban had not been among those who greeted me in the corridor. He sat there, at the window, with knitted eyebrows, watching us filing in. There was something strange about him. It took me a little time to realise what it was. He let the others overwhelm me with questions, asking such things as whether I had anything to eat during the past day, whether I had found the people I knew in Pau and if so, why couldn't they help me to get over to Lourdes? I told them that I had eaten, that I had stayed with the person I had been looking for and that I had no opportunity to travel, since I couldn't ask him for money, and that I had tried to walk to Lourdes but I got into a car that took me back to Pau. Now Father Esteban said:

" It was very foolish of you to be left behind!"

Only now did I realise what was so unusual about him. He did not smile. He looked grave, like a teacher looks at a pupil who has violated the rules. I stared at him. Father Anselmo said:

" Of course you don't know."

" What don't I know?" I asked.

" We have witnessed a great miracle."

They all chimed in, eager to tell me of the great miracle

that had happened to Father Esteban at Lourdes. It transpired that they went to the Grotto of the Blessed Virgin to pray and then Father Esteban was led to the holy piscine to bathe in its wondrous waters. The rest of them had gone to the subterranean cathedral, leaving Father Esteban in the care of one of those good people who help the ailing.

When he joined them again, they saw him coming towards them and then, as if he had seen a divine apparition, he fell on his knees, and when he was helped to his feet, shaken and trembling, he was a changed man.

They were so overcome with the wonder of Father Esteban's experience, that my own mishap had been forgotten. Imagine coming to Lourdes and partaking in a real miracle.

I remembered Father Esteban as a cheerful, smiling, good-natured fellow, tending his flowers, saying little, but bursting with goodwill and I was over-awed by the change in him. Not that he showed himself unkind to me. On the contrary, he suggested putting my name up once more for a pilgrimage and offered to explain to the abbot my ill-luck in missing my train. But he didn't seem to be the same Father Esteban I had loved so much before the miracle had happened to him.

We reached Hendaye by eleven a.m. and had to tramp to passport control and customs while our carriage was shifted to the platform from which trains left for Spain. The carabinero stood lazily at the gate, rifle on his shoulder, revolver in his holster, grim, unsmiling. His officer stamped my passport mechanically, his face rather handsome, clean-shaven, with probing eyes, solemn and silent.

No, he had no warrant to arrest me. Perhaps he will receive his orders after we have gone, just when the train steams out of the station. He'll be annoyed to have missed me and to have missed a good opportunity to show his efficiency. In years to come, he will be still a lieutenant and he will attribute the lack of advancement to the fact that he failed to hold that priest who had betrayed his country, plotted with an enemy of the State, and helped " public enemy number one " to defy the law.

We travelled through the sun-drenched landscape of Spain. Father Anselmo undid the basket which contained the left-overs of the food the cook in the seminary had prepared for us. The bread was a little stale, crumbling all over our tunics, the sausage warm, its skin soaked with fat. Father Esteban complained about not wrapping greaseproof paper around it. He assured us that now that *he* was taking over once more the planning and the books in the seminary, such would not be the case in the future.

At every station where our train stopped, I expected a carabinero to open the door and call my name. But though there were carabineros at every station, none had opened the door and none had called my name. It got very hot. Father Vicente pulled down the window and grumbled about the soot which had been absent on the French railways as they had been electrified some time ago. Little black flakes started to float about. Soon, when you touched the door-handle, or your own suitcase, your hands got black with grimy smuts. Then, about the time when we passed through Erice, it began to get dark, one couldn't see the filth any more and it did not matter how dirty one got. In an hour we should be sitting in the bus sent by the seminary and a few minutes later we would be at home and could clean up and settle down to answer questions from those who had stayed behind.

Still, I might not get as far as that. It might be no bus for me, but the black van of the policia. The questions,

too, might be asked by somebody else, not by brother
priests in the seminary. I wondered if there was a bath in
the prison at the policia?

We arrived in Pamplona, only forty-eight hours after we
had left. It seemed an eternity. There were four carabineros promenading on the platform, in two pairs. One
of them turned after an old couple and called:

"Hey, you!"

The two old people went on towards the exit, not knowing that it was meant for them. The other pair of carabineros had waited near the barrier. The sergeant grabbed
the old man's arm.

"Can't you hear?"

The old man carrying a heavy sack on his shoulder
wondered: "Who would call me?"

"The police."

By now the first two men of the law had joined them.

"What's in the sack?"

"Sack," answered the old man and made to continue
towards the exit. The most suspicious carabinero shook his
head in despair.

"How stupid can one get?" It was a rhetorical question
addressed to the bystanders who always gather and are
always ready to laugh with the stronger. The carabinero
rather liked his own remark for he repeated it: "How
stupid can you get? I ask him what's in that sack and he
says: 'Sack.' Let me see."

The woman did not take part in the proceedings. She
just stared after the train which had begun to move away,
the engine spitting fire from its chimney. We stood, waiting
for the way to the exit to be cleared, nobody complaining
or caring, most of us glad not to have missed this free
entertainment.

The old man dumped the sack on the platform under the station clock, the carabinero cut the string that closed the neck of the sack, and buried both hands in it. When he brought them up, they held a neat pile of folded sacks. Some laughed, but no one dared to laugh too long about the carabinero's blunder. The sacks were thrown on the floor, the old man called his wife and both started to fold them and put them back where they had come from. The four carabineros marched away with measured steps. They seemed to guard nothing but their own dignity.

The small crowd moved forward again.

The bus was there, the driver told us that last night a huge thunderstorm had swept over Pamplona, causing a deluge in the city, washing away everything that could be moved, damaging the awnings of cafés and shops.

" But there's no damage to Father Esteban's flowers. I've just seen them. The Lord has protected them."

He expected an acknowledgement from Father Esteban. Probably not more than the usual benevolent smile. But there was no smile, only a curt remark from Father Esteban.

" You talk too much."

The driver had not heard of Father Esteban's miracle, and so he wondered, stowed away the few pieces of luggage, climbed behind the wheel, and let in the clutch. Determined to impress us with his news, he switched to a new subject.

" And the greatest news is that an epidemic has broken out. Nobody knows what it is yet, but there is a rumour it might be smallpox. The Santa Cruz hospital is closed to the public."

Almost everybody had gone to bed when we drove through the main gate. But Father Xavier was still awake. Not because he wished to stay up to greet us, but because once .woken up, he couldn't fall asleep for hours. The

secretary, whose duty it was to await our arrival, stood at
the entrance, flanked by the night porter. Of course the
great news was the miracle of Father Esteban. It spread
like wildfire. Many got out of bed as soon as they heard
of it, to listen to it again and again, to touch him, to ask
him for the smallest details. The abbot had come down, in
his tidy, rather worldly, dressing-gown, and ordered a short
impromptu service in the chapel to offer our thanks to the
Lord for the grace received by Father Esteban.

The centre of all this fuss, Father Esteban himself,
seemed a trifle gloomy. He looked blank when one of the
fathers mentioned his flowers. Without showing the slightest interest, he turned to the abbot who had changed
hastily into his vestments, telling him that he intended to
take control of the accounts once again and the very next
day.

We lighted our candles and filed into the chapel. I asked
Father Xavier about the hospital. He had not been called
out once while I was away. He, too, had heard of the
rumour of an epidemic and was glad not to have had to go
there. He worried about his own health and regarded me
with suspicion, for I, too, had been in the hospital Friday
evening. I told him that I went only to the women's ward.
The epidemic might have broken out in the men's ward.
Anyway, nothing seemed wrong with me though Father
Xavier thought he could detect a paleness in my face and
thought that my forehead felt hot.

Kneeling on the cool stone floor of the chapel made me
feel better. I had come home, having done what my
conscience bade me. Here I was and everything had turned
out reasonably well. To-morrow I would ask permission
to go to confession and confession would lighten my
burden.

Then I saw the night porter in the door. I knew immediately that his appearance concerned me. He wouldn't have come to disturb the service in chapel, unless he had some very urgent reason to do so. He stood there, vaguely, his eyes searching for someone until they found me. The secretary went over to him, they whispered for a moment, then both went out together. A minute later the secretary returned, tiptoed to me and asked me to go with him.

Pacing up and down in front of the announcement board near the porter's lodge, Lieutenant Zapater waited in the hall, richly attired with polished leather belt, shoulder-strap, the insignia of police officers, which caught the only light burning, each time he passed a certain point on the marble floor. When he saw us, he stopped. He sounded efficient and polite.

" You are Father Francisco." It was not a question. It was a statement. " We met on Friday evening, I believe."

I nodded and he went on explaining. " Captain Viñolas would like to have a word with you, Father."

The secretary wanted to know what it was all about and if it could not wait till morning. But the officer remained adamant. It had to be now, forthwith, immediately. The police thought I might help clear up a rather important matter, something that could not brook delay. The secretary played for time, he said he had to report it to the abbot, hinting that the abbot might get in touch with the bishop. Lieutenant Zapater parried it skilfully. It was a small matter, he would bring me back in no time. Before we left, he had another request. He asked permission to take the typewritten sheet on the notice board with him. It was the notice giving the names of the six priests who were selected to go on the pilgrimage to Lourdes, this past week-end. It included my name.

Zapater drove himself. He was a cautious driver, flashing his headlights at every corner and slowing down almost to a standstill. He drove straight to the policia, parked the car and led me to the main gate. We passed the big, glass-covered frames in which posters of lost property and wanted criminals were displayed for all to see, offering rewards, requesting the general public's assistance in maintaining the law. I tried to look away when we brushed past the poster which showed the photograph of Manuel Artiguez. " 100,000 Pesos!" it said. " Dead or alive." " 100,000 Pesos to anyone who supplies information leading to the arrest of Manuel Artiguez." I saw Zapater watching me.

When we entered through the small gate, the policeman on duty stopped Zapater, drawing him aside. It was obviously something very urgent. Though they spoke in whispers, I could hear clearly what they were saying. Captain Viñolas had left to follow up a report, Lieutenant Zapater was to proceed as fast as he could to the Calle de la Cruz.

" What has happened?" asked an astonished Zapater.

" We have had a report that Artiguez, the bandit, has been seen."

" Where?"

" Here, in Pamplona."

7

THE TRAIN had gone and with it the little priest. Francisco was his name and they called him Father Francisco. He didn't look to me like "Father", he looked to me just Francisco. All the same, he added up to something. I hoped he wouldn't get into trouble with Viñolas. But priests were safe in Spain. After all, they were on the same side as the police. When I raided the church, nineteen months ago, the police were there to kill us. I got two bullets and I can't move my head very well even now. In turn, the priests were praying in their churches for the security of the Government and for the safety of the police, and preached to all fools of worshippers that salvation lay in prayers, in praising goodness, in condemning evil and, of course, priests were good and we were evil.

There was nothing much happening in Pau on any morning. On a Sunday morning there was even less. I took the funicular, the conductor blew his whistle and we glided up the Boulevard. There were two children in the carriage, not more than four and six, both girls, running wildly about, as if they owned the place. Their parents, loaded with a pram and several large and small pieces of luggage, were trying to cope with them, but the brats, sensing that authority didn't function in funiculars as

efficiently as at home, seemed to take not the slightest
notice. Now, Spanish children would be better behaved.
A Spanish father would raise his voice only once and the
child would know that the next thing would be a good,
smart smacking. But these French fathers—holy smoke!
And just look at him, carrying even his wife's handbag,
while she puts on more paint or powder or what not on her
face. We wouldn't load more on a donkey in Spain, and
heaven knows we know how to load our donkeys. Those
donkeys of Francisco's father! There's a strange story for
you. Killed in the war and having no idea by which side.

A flood of water was running along the Boulevard,
turned on by the sweepers. On weekdays they turn it off
much earlier, but on Sunday they let it cascade till as late as
nine-thirty and later. We never do it in Spain, water being
much too precious. When I was a boy, I got out one of our
donkeys one Sunday morning, while my father was still
sleeping, and filled up the water-skins at San Isidoro's well
outside the village, a well which everybody knew to be the
best in the district. Nobody ever used the water from that
well for washing, it was good for drinking, good even for
mixing with wine. One Sunday morning, I could make
a whole peseta from selling it. But when my father found
out, he beat me hard and took away all the money I had
made that Sunday. He said he thrashed me because I had
harnessed the donkey, though I should have remembered
that the donkey had worked all week, just as hard as he
himself, just as *he* needed a day of rest, so did the donkey.
I didn't mind the thrashing, because my father had given
me the reason why he did it. A good smack doesn't do
any harm to a boy, but he must know the reason for it.

I wondered if Pablo minded me slapping his face yesterday? Well, there was not much reason for that. He

seemed rather sulky about it even when I tried to make up
with him. But children don't bear ill-will for long. If you
ask me, he had forgotten it already. He liked his new
football. It will give him prominence among the children
in the Spanish Street. They will listen to what he says, he
will set up new rules about playing the game, and he will
tell them that anyone who calls Manuel Artiguez a " mighty
mouse " will be left out of the teams playing with the new
football. Or, perhaps, they'll change Pablo to one of their
own kind and he'll tell them from first-hand knowledge
that I behaved like a coward when I heard that Pilar was
ill and wanted to see me before she died. Perhaps Pablo,
too, will scribble nasty things on the walls about me and
pull faces when I walk down the street. What a pity that
one never knows how things are going to turn out. If I
had known that Carlos was an informer and Viñolas wanted
to trap me in the hospital of Santa Cruz in Pamplona, I
could have shown all the courage in the world, knowing
that I'd be warned in time and wouldn't have to go anyway.

I stood on the pavement in the Boulevard des Pyrénées,
looking across the valley, the water cascading under my
feet. The mountains showed up clearly. With a little
imagination you could even see the green shadows on the

slopes. That was, of course, the forest, reaching up to the
snow-line. How often I had trod among those trees,
strong and free, like a tiger in the jungle, not dreading to
meet anybody or anything, knowing that everybody was
dreading meeting me.

I walked the empty streets, towards a street, a short one,
which I knew had a bistro at one end, called Le Navarre.
In that street lived one of my friends. The bistro was open,
a one-eyed waiter splashed water among the iron tables
and mopped the pavement under the chairs. I ordered a
carafe of " *blanc* " and two hard-boiled eggs and asked him
if he knew a man called Dages who had a Spanish boy,
called Pablo, living with him? The waiter knew the name.
Several people had inquired about somebody called Dages
lately. But he did not know in which house they lived.
So I sat there for a while, hoping that Pablo would come
down and we would be friends again.

Across the place, I could see the range of mountains.
There, somewhere, a young man—less than half my age—
was climbing to escape the rage of Manuel Artiguez and
just as well, for if I caught up with him, I would break his
neck with my bare hands. I felt satisfaction in knowing
Carlos was terrified of me. It was nice to know that somebody was. The children in the Spanish Street weren't.
Pablo wasn't. Francisco wasn't either. Of course Pablo and
Francisco were friends and they knew I wouldn't harm them.

I ate the hard-boiled eggs and ordered a " bock " and
then a large beer. The one-eyed waiter brought them, he
was anxious to start a conversation, but I didn't much care
to converse with a one-eyed waiter and sent him on his
way to fetch some more eggs. He saw a van stopping and
said that the man in it knew Dages. A young fellow climbed
out, with a little moustache, a cigarette dangling under it,

in soft, crêpe-soled shoes, so that you couldn't hear when
he walked. He came over. While he talked to the one-eyed
waiter, I tried to read the words on the van. I took out
my glasses and read: " Marcel Bonnier, *Négociant en Vins,*
St. Etienne-de-Baigorry. B.-Pyr." That was the place
where Pedro lived. Or near it, anyway. Having heard
what the one-eyed waiter had to say, Crêpe-soles joined me,
asking politely if he could do so? Soon I knew that he
was the fellow who had brought Pablo to Pau and a great
friend of my own friend, Pedro. He was driving back to
St. Etienne this morning and as he had heard the day before
that Pablo was missing, he wanted to find out, before he
got on his way, if the boy had turned up all right. I told
him that Pablo was well and safe and also that Pedro had
gone back to his gloomy wife. The mention of a woman
brought out a great sigh from Marcel. I asked him what
he wanted to drink, he ordered Jurançon and I had another
large beer and when he repeated the order, we agreed that
Pau looked empty and boring on Sunday. I wanted to see
a friend and as I could not see my friend, Pablo, the right
thing to do was to see my other friend, Pedro. Marcel
would be glad to have company, we would stop for lunch
outside Oloron and I could be at Pedro's before the day
was out.

Never once did he ask me who I was. He drove fast,
talked a lot, mainly about women as Frenchmen always do.
I liked him in spite of his crêpe-soled shoes and little
moustache. He liked my friends Pedro and Pablo and that
was good enough for me.

He stopped at a riverside restaurant for lunch. The
owner knew him well, a fat, clean-shaven fellow, the sort
whom you don't dare to ask what is cooking in the kitchen,
who knew everything better than anybody else, including

F

what you wanted to eat. He had a hobby of making baskets
of piano wires, but, he said, he had already made so many
different baskets that there were no artistic problems left
in basket making, so he had started a new hobby: mosaic
making. He brought along a few examples of his new
hobby, a table with a mosaic top, a tray, inlaid with little
stones. He spoke a little Spanish, showing off with it,
making remarks he thought funny about Marcel. We had
to go to see a second-hand car he had bought the other day
and he and Marcel started a discussion on the merits of
second-hand cars, how much it mattered that a car should
have had only one owner, low mileage and such things as
whether the car was kept in a garage.

A waitress brought trout, she said they were caught in
the river at the bottom of the garden. She was a young
girl, overworked, with sweat-patches in her armpits, her
brassière, too, got saturated with perspiration, her young
breasts showing through in a most alarming way. Marcel
spoke to her and laughed, but she didn't like what he said,
her face flushed with embarrassment and when she took
the trout bones, she refused to come back and serve us,
and the fat patron who made mosaics had to bring our
chicken himself. She went on serving the other guests,
avoiding coming face to face with Marcel, but I could see
her, behind Marcel's back, sweating away, carrying trays of
dishes, and her hard little breasts, which looked even more
alarming when she turned away in an attempt to hide them.

I thought I was immune in these matters. I tried not to
think of it. I forced myself to turn my thoughts to Pedro.
He *will be* surprised to see me. I'll be there for dinner, his
gloomy woman must be preparing it now. After dinner,
when she leaves us to ourselves, I can ask him about some
little place, not far from his own. We might be neighbours

and I could come over to see him almost every night and we could talk about things of the past and the gloomy woman could bring us wine when we had finished the bottle. In winter there would be a fire of logs, probably spruce, the kind that burns with bouquets of sparks which you could watch for a long time when you wished to stop talking. I would have, of course, a big fire, too. I'd cut the logs myself in the backyard. In spring we'd go fishing, Pedro and I, he had that place on the Gave and kept the fishing-rights, not for the reason of fishing, but because he didn't want strangers trespassing on his land on account of our Thompsons being buried there. I'd invite Pablo, too. I'd teach him to fish, but more likely than not, he knew already. Every Spanish boy in the north knows how to fish. José Dages had probably taken his boy on fishing-trips in the mountains many times. Pablo could come in the winter, too, sit with us in front of the fire, or watch me making a sledge for him. The foot-hills are just right to play with a sledge. I could start all sorts of hobbies like this fat chap who makes baskets of piano-wire and those mosaic trays.

I had an argument with Marcel over who paid the bill and while he wandered over to greet some people he knew, I went inside to find the patron and pay. I found the girl in the cool inner room, struggling with a bottle, trying to pull out a stubborn cork. She smiled at me and straightened up as I took the bottle from her to help her. I pulled and pulled without making the slightest impression on that blasted cork. I pulled and dragged and jerked and wrenched, watching disappointment appear on her shiny little face. She laughed and wanted to have the bottle back and to have another go herself. I had never wanted so much to pull a cork. Manuel Artiguez defeated by a bloody cork. Manuel Artiguez, the lion-hearted, the savage, the brute,

struggling with a cork in front of a girl. I tore at it with
a swelling rage and, suddenly, it flew out like a shot,
splashing red wine all over her blouse and my trousers.
She laughed again, then, realising the damage I had
suffered, she grabbed a napkin, soaking it with water from a
jug, and started furiously rubbing the spots. I still held the
bottle with aching fingers, watching her kneeling in front
of me, with her flowing hair, softly arching back,
tight skirt and brown calves. I put down the bottle, wiped
the sticky red wine from my hands with her napkin and
pulled her up so that her body brushed against mine. She
got very frightened and I let her go. She was in such a
hurry that she forgot the bottle, but she looked back from
the kitchen door and smiled. I went out into the garden.
Marcel had got hold of the patron and was paying the bill.

I felt young and reckless and did not mind Marcel
driving like a lunatic and turning after every skirt that
happened to pass us. He took a side road before we got to
St. Etienne, cut through some fields, crossed a bridge and
deposited me in front of Pedro's house. I thanked him and
promised to call on him before I went back to Pau. The
next moment he was off, careering down the lane towards
the bridge.

The roses smelt heavy. Yellow, pink and red petals lay
in thick layers on the path. The green shutters were closed
against the burning afternoon sun, but the door was open.
I went inside, stopped to get my eyes used to the half-
light of the parlour. Upstairs, in the bathroom, the water
was rushing into the tub. I called, but got no answer. So
I went up the stairs. The bathroom door was ajar, behind
it there was light and movement. I did not call again, but
stepped forward and saw on the tiled wall the reflection of
a woman, ready to step into the tub, bending down to test

the water. Blood raced up to my head. She had a worn face, but her skin was young and firm and little used like a practically new second-hand car with very low mileage and with one single owner who kept it most of the time in the garage and drove it only on rare occasions. She was very strong, but I felt stronger than ten of her kind and twenty of her husband's kind. I felt the sparks of blazing spruce in my blood. She fought me but she had not a chance.

Neither had I.

Pedro had been drinking the whole blessed day in the garden of the bistro. The lights were switched on, though it was not really dark yet. I saw the patron waving to me as I hurried past. I had no stomach either for his wine or for his talk. I just wanted to get out of the place, take a bus, hire a car, or walk until I dropped. The patron went inside and told Pedro he had seen me and Pedro came running after me. He seemed pretty drunk, but being drunk made him even happier to see me. He asked when I arrived and what the news was and I answered only his second question, telling him about Carlos, lying that I had come to find the bloody traitor before he had a chance to cross the border. Pedro insisted on coming with me, put his arms around me, partly out of affection and partly because he couldn't stand on his feet otherwise. He dragged me into the bistro, we had a very quick bottle of red wine under trees lit up by clusters of electric bulbs hidden in the foliage. He insisted on introducing me to everyone as his very best friend. In fact, I had never seen him so utterly drunk before. He kept on telling me that I must go home with him to have dinner, though his wife disliked me lately on account of thinking that I had persuaded her husband to come with

me to Spain. I thought: she liked me all right. Not at
first perhaps, but later she did. I could tell she did. But
I told him that I wouldn't go home with him just now, for
I had to go after Carlos who most probably wouldn't bother
to stop for dinner, but would try to slip over to Spain as
fast as he could. I said to Pedro:

" You can't come with me, you're drunk."

He burst into tears and told everybody that although
I hurt him, I was his best friend and he would do anything
to please me, including going home to sleep off his
intoxication.

I had Pedro's gun and four cartridges in it. When I
reached the edge of the forest, I knew Pedro must have
reached the little house with the green shutters, the rose
petals on the paving and the woman who would never again
leave the door open while she was taking her bath as long
as she lived. I wondered where he would find her? Would
she still be upstairs, or did she go down? Was she preparing dinner, or would it be the first time that her husband
had come home and no dinner had been waiting for him?
Would he understand what she told him, or would he
just topple over and she would have to drag him to bed as
she had done so often in the past, undressing him and
tucking him in, listening to his snoring and smelling his evil
breath all night.

I started to climb under the trees, higher and higher. It
surprised me how well I climbed. No fatigue, not much
noise from the lungs—not much as yet, anyway. My legs
got the idea first. The brain caught up with them only
a little later. The brain wanted to go anywhere where
I wouldn't meet Pedro, or his hard-faced wife with the
surprisingly young body. The legs knew exactly where to

go. No more little house for me, no more fire with flying
sparks and endless tittle-tattle in front of it. I wasn't made
for that sort of life. I was made to *do* things, not to talk
about them. Pilar was dead. Why the blazes didn't I go
to see her in time? It can't be helped. I'm going now,
I'll see her just as well as I would have seen her two days
ago. She wouldn't have told me much even if I had arrived
in time. She would have scolded me most probably for
one thing or another, why hadn't I worn my glasses or
why hadn't I shaved and why wouldn't I take a wife and
suchlike. Just as well she hadn't said all these things.
I had heard them often enough before. Pilar, too, was a
person who rather *did* things. I was going to see her now,
and I might catch up with Carlos before he could tell
Viñolas about Francisco.

There was a full moon above the trees, climbing in
company with me, the moon among the branches and I
beneath. There comes a time in a man's life when he loses
the companionship of everyone. Only things like the moon
and like one's memories are left. On second thoughts,
not even memories lasted. Mine were fading rapidly. There
were people whose lot was climbing all the way. Others
just coasted down the slope. I had had to climb all my
life. Pedro was the coasting type. So was Marcel. But
Francisco you could call the trudging type. Francisco and
I belonged to the same pattern. Worriers, always wanting
to do things the hard way. Why had he chosen to be
mixed up with me? And why am I going to Pamplona
now, trying to save him?

It was now ten-thirty. I forced myself to climb for
another quarter of an hour. That would bring me to the
border. It ran in a narrow valley covered with bramble,
full of large boulders, smooth on one side and mossy on the

other. The part of descending I hated more than climbing.
The foot was less sure when stumbling down, and one
made much more noise. When I reached the first boulder,
I was just about done in. I slumped down like a heavy
sack of misery. I chose this part for no patrol could
negotiate such stony narrows by night. A patrol always
consisted of more than one carabinero and one of them
would surely be inferior to the others, sliding on the slippery
side of the boulders, slipping on the sharp stones, making
a noise and so endangering the safety of the whole patrol.

I sat with my back leaning against that boulder, breathing
with open month, to make less noise, my eyes closed, all
my senses focused through my ears. Then the exhaustion
slowly receded, the heart began to pound less heavily, the
breeze managed to dry the sweat on my face, I opened my
eyes. The moon hid behind the range above me, just at the
back of the spur of the highest trees, throwing an aura of
silver over them. Not a single cloud in the sky. I thought
how chancy it would be to cross the plateau leading to the
slope which slid down to Elizondo. It had no trees at all
and in light like this, throwing sharper shadows than the
afternoon sun, it seemed suicide. The best plan was to get
on the road, hold up a vehicle of some kind, and force the
driver to take me to Pamplona. You had to have sharp
eyes, though, in choosing the car. I remembered how, in
1951, when Pedro, the two gipsies and I stopped a van,
it turned out to be an army van, coming back from
Dancharinea, having taken twenty-two carabineros there.
It only had two guards and we killed both with knives, so
that we had made no unnecessary noise.

My thoughts stopped dead. Somebody, not a hundred
yards away, blew a whistle. I eased Pedro's little automatic
from my pocket, making less noise than the shadow of a

ghost. There it was again, a soft whistle, not meant to carry far, advertising the fact that the man it was meant for, shouldn't be far away. Someone slid down from the other side, cautiously, but foolishly all the same. As soon as he got a foothold, he held his breath for a while and then blew the whistle again. Now another whistle answered him.

It took them a little while to find each other. Still with some bramble between them, one whispered:

" What the black devil made you wander away?"

The other broke through the last bit of thorn, just the opposite side of my boulder, and the two were now together. They sounded fed up, but not frightened. The caution they exercised was not all due to the man they hunted, but to the fact that they wanted to avoid being overheard by their officer. The one who spoke had a thick-throated voice, keeping it well down to a mutter. His chum was out of breath, blowing like a rusty ventilator.

" Had to step behind a tree. When I had finished, the whole lot of you had gone. I couldn't call, I couldn't light my torch, what am I supposed to do, follow you by scent?"

I could hear him dropping his rifle beside him. The other fellow, too, slipped off his. I could hear him leaning it against the boulder, but it slipped and settled next to the first. This was the chance for me, I could easily creep around and hit one of them somewhere where it hurt, terrify the second into silence and knife him without either of them uttering a single sound. Then I would have two rifles and two corpses and two of their whistles, approach the rest, blow the whistle, lure them, one by one, away from the patrol and finish them off piecemeal. But what good would that do to-night? I had to get to Pamplona as fast as I could and there was no point in wasting time here, where something could have easily gone wrong. They might have another patrol nearby, with machine-guns and walkie-talkies, raise the whole bloody frontier, warn the road patrols, alert all police-posts, halt every car, block every way.

" He said he'd put you in irons," replied one of the two.

" Did he?" There was irony in his voice. " What would he do if I slipped over the border? Just a few steps and I could tell him: go and sleep with your mother."

" Shhh!"

They listened. There was absolutely nothing to be heard, except the usual sounds of the night. The dark wing-beat of a bird in its nest, adjusting its balance. The occasional falling of a leaf from the foliage of a tree on either slope. The darting of a field-mouse from one shadow to another. But, of course, no carabinero would hear things like that.

" Oh, nothing," said the tired one. " You want us to go and find them?"

" No. Let's get our breath back first." He sighed. " I wish I were back home."

" Where's that?"

There came another sigh. " Arrieta. In bed with the wife. Warm as toast. Only softer. You married?"

" Uhm."

" She warm?"

" Uhm."

" The angels save you from a cold wife. One who wants *you* to warm *her*. Her feet like concrete. Her fingers like icicles. Her breast like an iceberg."

The other spat. " Two icebergs."

Right at my toes a ball of thorns began to stir, changed shape, became a huge potato sprouting into all directions, and turned out to be a hedgehog. It made its way across the dry undergrowth, breaking little branches and dehydrated leaves while moving. At once the hoarse-voiced man got alarmed.

" Psst!"

" That was something," agreed his pal.

" Not a person. A snake."

The hedgehog scurried into the jungle of brambles.

" I'm terrified of snakes. I loathe them like sin. Do you?"

" It *is* a snake. One of those short ones. I know snakes."

The other man raised his rifle from the ground. " Let's go."

The first soldier took pleasure in teasing him. " Not yet. Let us see that snake."

" You can see it on your own. I'm clearing out of here."

I watched the hedgehog melting into the vegetation. First its shape went, then the movement of the undergrowth ceased, and then the noise died, too. The frightened man pleaded: " Let's go. He'll be furious. Nothing frightens me more than snakes."

I thought what would you do if you'd come round this boulder and seen Manuel Artiguez with this little metal tool in his hand pointing at the spot between your eyes? You'd make your pants full, though you had just been behind that tree. I heard the other getting his rifle, throwing it over his shoulder. The same moment, they and I heard a new whistle calling. The thick-voiced fellow whispered:

" There they are. We'll get it now, both."

The other muttered back: " We'll say we've heard something. We thought it was *him*."

One of them blew his whistle. The answer came immediately. They trotted off towards it.

The moon had risen now above the spine of the trees, and,
suddenly, there was a flock of small clouds, followed by a
large dark one which seemed to drive them towards the
lighted disc. Luck had not deserted me. When the big
cloud wrapped itself around the moon, I started. I went
back to the French side and followed the narrow valley
under the trees, treading on soft turf all the time. When
I could hear the waterfall, I crossed over and started to
climb. The roaring of the water made it unnecessary to
tread softly. Only my eyes had to be careful now. I felt
no tiredness at all. I reached the top in a few minutes,
descended swiftly, still with the waterfall in my ears, found
that I had come a little too much to the left, for the light
of the forestry-hut appeared too much on my right. When
the slope became really steep, I could see the road on the
opposite side, carved in the mountain. I stopped. The
lights of two cars were travelling towards the border, close
together. They must have been carabineros' cars, since
private drivers hated to follow each other so closely and
the road here was straight and wide enough to overtake.

The brook at the bottom lay in the shade, I waited a
minute, but nothing had stirred. I threw a stone into the
water and then another. No one moved. I stepped into the
cold stream and got wet up to the knee. Ten minutes
later I hit the road. I walked along it to the bend and
waited. A lorry came from Elizondo. Wrong direction.
The lorry made a hell of a noise, making it quite impossible
to hear any other vehicle. But a second later, it hooted
and another hooted back from the other side of the bend.
Now I saw its headlights. It wasn't a van, it looked like a

private car. Should I step forward? I hesitated before jumping into the cone of the light and then it was too late. The car raced past. I saw the banner of the policia on the car's nose. Four men were sitting in it, driving as fast as you could under the circumstances. Three of them were in uniform. The fourth had no hat on and I could have sworn it was Carlos.

Another minute crept by as I stood there, blinded by rage and the urge to find out. I heard another car climbing up from Elizondo and stepped on the crown of the road, waving, cursing and roaring. The car came from the bend, its lights hit me, the driver jammed on the brakes and stopped, skidding a metre or two sideways. In a way it was lucky to have stopped a car going the wrong way, for in this way, I had the seat next to the driver nearest to me and could jump in, in the shortest possible time, without having to go round the nose of the car. Not knowing how to drive, I had to rely on persuading the driver to do what I wanted him to do. I tore open the door and saw that the man was alone. A young man, very frightened, a sort of delivery man, with a pencil behind his ear and terror in his eyes. I told him to turn round and fast, or I would throw him over the railings into the river. He obeyed all right, but had to shift the car to and fro several times. It seemed an eternity till he managed to turn with me watching the road in both directions, my eyes scanning the bends left and right. At last he had done it. He understood that I wanted him to take me to Pamplona without fuss and as fast as possible.

" Which church do you go to on Sundays?" I asked him.

" The one in Elizondo." He watched me from the corner of his eyes and I knew the moment when he recognised me. " I won't give you away, Señor Artiguez." His voice

trembled, though he tried to show himself brave. " I go
to church only to please my girl," he added and spoilt my
good impression of him.

" I want you to catch up with that car there." I showed
him the car in front of us, far ahead, when it became
visible for a moment on the serpentine. He tried, but he
couldn't do it. The other car was much faster. He
couldn't gain on it while descending and was hopelessly
left behind when climbing. I asked for his name.

" Lopez, Señor. Luis Lopez."

" What do you do?"

" I work for Miguel Cardenas. General merchandise and
delicatessen."

" Where?"

" Elizondo, Señor Artiguez. He's a bad man. A moneylender. He keeps bags of money hidden in his shop. You
know, for emergency. For people who must have money
at a moment's notice, when it doesn't matter how much
they pay for it. I know where he keeps the lot."

He looked long at me. I told him to shut up and keep
his eyes on the road. I asked him which street Cardenas's
shop was in, and made him avoid it. I let him pass through
the square where the policia stood, but I couldn't discover
the car I wanted to catch up with. They must have gone
straight through to Pamplona.

By 11.15, we drove into the outskirts of the city, the
Avenida del General Franco. We used to think that these
new name-plates of streets would have no time to rust on
the walls, but they did rust, having been up now for more
than twenty years. I wanted to go to the Plaza del Castillo,
but the young fool had no idea of the way. So I made
him turn into the Calle de la Media Luna, and then cross
the Arrieta. He knew the Bull Ring, of course, he came

often to watch corridas. He was one of those idiots who always watch others and never do anything on their own.

I got out of Luis Lopez's car just before we reached Castillo, he thanked me, the fool, and when I asked him for what, he started to stammer. I suppose he never expected to get away unharmed. I told him that I didn't mind him, or anybody else going to church on Sundays and, as a matter of fact, I had some friends among priests myself. He laughed foolishly, thinking that I was joking. I warned him not to tell anybody that he had met me, or I would find him at Cardenas's General Merchandise and strangle him with my bare hands. He promised on the holiness of the Holy Virgin not to breathe a word, and to return at once to Elizondo, but I knew his kind. If he doesn't go to Viñolas straight away, he'll wake up his girl or his moneylender master to brag about his news. I saw him starting towards the Plaza de Toros, stop, look back to see whether I was watching him, and when he could not discover me, he turned into the Avenida de Carlos III which leads to the policia, near the Plaza del General Mola.

A few seconds later I passed Santa Cruz and the entrance of the street with the hospital. Women's ward left, men's ward right. Nothing was wrong with my memory at all. The street seemed all right, too. I couldn't discover anything extraordinary, it seemed quite empty. There was the bank at the corner, the shutters down, there was a clock over the entrance just as Pablo remembered it. I wondered what Pablo was doing? Lying in bed, perhaps he couldn't sleep, perhaps he was thinking of me. Or he might be sleeping and dreaming of me, doing something big, like twisting Viñolas's ears. I thought of Viñolas, too. He might be talking to Carlos just about now. The bloody traitor will have told him by now that there was no use in waiting for me, the game was up, I had been warned. And Viñolas would get very angry, throw him out and give him nothing, except a kick in his arse and Carlos would starve to death, for he wouldn't dare to return to France where I had many sympathisers, and he wouldn't want to remain in Spain either, for a traitor has a miserable existence even if he had plenty of money, and without money his life was not worth living.

The intense light of the travel bureau made me quicken my steps. I couldn't afford to be recognised now. I saw the painted posters of Pau and Lourdes. Well, Francisco didn't get to Lourdes, but I did. That's life for you. Now we are both in Pamplona. That's life, too. It might be death.

Now then, here was a parallel street. Nothing much here either. An ambulance at the back entrance to the hospital—quite normal. On the opposite side a woman and a man were coming towards me, middle-aged people, harmless. I went on, skirted the square, stopped opposite the travel bureau and pondered. Where would Viñolas expect me to come from? Probably from either of the two streets from which the hospital could be reached. Would he expect me to come from a house in the square? Not likely. So, from there I should come.

I crossed the square and walked slowly along the houses on both sides of the travel office. I wanted to read the name-plates of the tenants, but I couldn't without glasses. Well, all evil has a good side to it—Francisco would say. I wonder how many people would recognise me with these specs on? I wouldn't. And specs are good, not only to disguise you, but they also give you the chance to read things. Now, let's see. A lawyer, a dentist, another dentist, Señora Martinez. No good. The next house: Dr. M.

Humez, physician. He had two bells, one for the night, the other for the day. C. Carreras, J. Carreras. That's the right house for me. I'll ring the doctor's day bell. Someone will open the door, I'll say I made a mistake, I want to go to C. Carreras. Right, here I go.

I could hear the bell. It did not sound far away at all. Just above me. But, except for the sound, there was no reaction to it at all. I tried it again—nothing. I was just about to press the doctor's night bell, when a car stopped, a little man jumped out, locked the car door and asked me:

" You want me? I'm the doctor."

I explained that I wished to see my friend, Carreras. He turned the key, let me enter first and pressed the automatic light button. We walked to the stairs together, but he was in a hurry and ran up the stairs like a monkey on a tree, calling back:

" You'll find your way. I have another call to make."

I heard him opening and slamming his door. I mounted to the top on the creaking stairs and stretched out my hand towards the trap-door, when the light went out. The stairs were too noisy to risk descending and searching for the light button. I tried to push up the trap-door, but it wouldn't budge. What the hell could be the matter with it? I couldn't remember any lock on it, just this handle. I was pushing with all my might *upwards*, heaving, panting, groaning. Miguel Moreno was the name of that silly old fool who used to boast of his strength. Women's ward left, men's ward right—nothing wrong with my memory, but, oh bloody hell, everything was wrong with my strength, like it was with Miguel Moreno's. Then suddenly the light came on again. I heard a door being slammed, it must have been the little doctor going out again. I examined the hinges closely and saw my mistake. I had to *pull* not *push*. Down it came, quite easily, with a collapsible ladder attached, held by a balancing mechanism. You could move it with one finger. The light went out again, but I didn't care now. I mounted and, gripping the uppermost step, pulled the ladder up so that it almost locked. In the loft I found a second ladder close by, and climbed up. This time one had to push to get on to the roof. There was a lot of light here, most of it from the street below, but also from the moon. I took my bearings. In front of me lay the square. That mass of light must belong to the travel bureau. There ran the Calle de la Cruz, the bank on the corner. It occurred to me that this would be the right way to rob the bank. Not now, though. Of course when they find out that I simply walked along the roofs, the bank might put a guard on the roof. Or put an alarm on the trap-door leading down to it. They might have one even now.

Not a sound here except the traffic below. The chimney-pots looked like mighty boulders, throwing weird shadows as I made my way among them, listening, spying the path to the next one. One, two, three—was this the hospital, or was it the next? Yes, this building continued into that wing on the parallel street. Now a sound startled me. Somebody, on the far side of this block of chimneys, started to whistle. He whistled softly. He whistled an old tune I knew well. Something about a melancholy woman who had been sent by her husband to market and never returned again to him. The husband searched for her, going to every market town on market days, asking everyone whether they had seen her, describing her sad face and never-smiling eyes. But no one had ever seen the sad-faced woman since, having left her dour, masterful husband, she never looked sad again, her eyes always smiled now, she became the lover of many fine men who didn't send their wives to market, but went themselves.

There was a noise on the street, a car and voices. Slowly, with the utmost caution, I crept to the edge of the chimney. From here I could see the man. His eyes were riveted on some windows on the opposite side of the street. He held in his lap a bulky object, wrapped in a rug, he wore the uniform of the policia, not very young, probably trained before the civil war. To kill one of these old-timers counted half a dozen of the new chaps. It was uncanny to see him not interested at all in what went on in the street. He just stared at those windows and nothing else. But I saw who arrived in the car. No one else but my special friend, Luis Lopez, from Cardenas's General Stores in Elizondo, escorted by two of Viñolas's officers. They took Luis inside. A few seconds later the heavy curtains over the windows of the third-floor flat were drawn aside and light blazed from them across the street.

Now I understood. This was a signal and the man on my roof had been waiting for it. He unwrapped the object in his lap, it turned out to be the finest damn' rifle I had ever seen, with short barrel and a first-class telescope mounted on it. He polished it and tried the lock, while I crept up to him. I hit him on the back of the neck with Pedro's automatic. I could have done it with my bare fist. With this hard metal, it was almost too much. He slumped forward, I gave him a kick and at the same time grabbed his rifle. But his cramped fingers were holding the rifle and I had to give it a twist before he went over the parapet. It seemed a long time before he hit the pavement with a

ghastly thud, right in front of the entrance to the hospital. Several men ran out, shouting. The blazing window opposite opened and two shapes appeared in it. The first was Viñolas. The second: one of his henchmen. What luck to see Viñolas just when I had this marvel of a gun. Pablo would like that. I got him in the telescopic sight. But now a third person joined them: Carlos. I hesitated for a heartbeat and thought. I might not have the chance of two shots. Which one would it be? I moved the telescope and I had them, one after the other, as large as life. Viñolas, the butcher. I returned to Carlos. Viñolas was an enemy. Carlos was a traitor. I pulled the trigger, he screamed and disappeared from my view. But he did not fall. He hung wedged in the corner of the window. The other two had dived out of sight.

Now then, I had to hurry.

A small light showed the open door to the inside of the hospital loft. I had a rifle with several more shots and also the little fellow in my other hand. I ran down the steps, just in time to see two carabineros climbing into the loft. One fired, but missed, then I fired twice. One of them had a submachine-gun. With great regret, I had to abandon my lovely rifle for that.

The stairs were empty, but lower down there was much commotion. I ran towards the landing. I went on repeating to myself: Left the women's ward, right the men's ward; left the women, right the men. Then I saw the signs: Bloody hell—it was the other way round. Left was the men's ward and right the women's. How silly, I thought, what does it matter that Pablo made a mistake, one simple mistake. Or was it *my* memory again? More likely. Much more likely.

I stood on the landing, for a second alone. Then they came. From the wards and from below, firing like lunatics. I saw a sign " Silence " shot to pieces. Then they got me. I

spun around from the force of the hits and, suddenly, the signs of the two wards were as they should have been all the time: the women's ward left, the men's right. Pablo had remembered them correctly after all. And nothing was wrong with my memory either. But something seemed to be all wrong with my strength.

8

CROUCHING under the window, I heard Sanchez saying:
"Are you all right, sir?"

I wasn't all right at all. My knees hurt and when I tried
to move, the right knee felt sheer agony. I must have
banged my legs while taking cover, against the lampstand,
and now couldn't move at all. Not that I wanted to move
with that beast covering us from wherever he was. He
got The Smuggler all right. We tried to pull him down
but he got pinioned between the window-sill and the desk.
Blood was dripping from his chest and Sergeant Sanchez
said he couldn't be helped and needed cover no more.

What was Vasquez, the sharp-shooter, doing? Surely
he must have seen where the shot came from. He had his
famous rifle with the telescopic sight. The man beside me
reasoned:

"That body that fell from the roof must have been

Vasquez, sir. Artiguez must be on the roof. And has the rifle."

Holy smoke, I must crawl away from here somehow. That idiotic youngster who brought the news that Artiguez had been seen, stood near the door, staring with open mouth at us. What a sight. The chief of police lying prostrate, with a damaged knee, while Manuel Artiguez is being cornered and destroyed. The battle had been joined at last and the general couldn't get on his feet. Then Sanchez called:

"You, lad, switch off the light."

I wished I had said that, the only sensible thing one could say under the circumstances.

"Just what I wanted to say," I heard myself agreeing. "And try the walkie-talkie, Sanchez."

The light went out, the sergeant got the walkie-talkie going. While he waited for an answer, he asked again:

"Are you hurt, sir?"

I explained my predicament to him, he began to massage my knee, but I had to stop him, it hurt so much. We got through to the ambulance filled with my men, and we had contact with the laundry van, also. I ordered the lot to converge on the main hospital building, to get the search-lights going, to sweep all the roofs with them. Then Zapater came through, reporting that from the top landing, from the staircase and from the landing which led to the wards, our men had cornered Artiguez. On the laundry roof, another battle had been going on, presumably with other members of the gang. I told him that, according to my information, Artiguez was on his own, and he went to investigate. It annoyed me no end that Zapater seemed to be right in the thick of it while I lay, out of action, under the window-sill with my knee hurting like hell.

Then it was all over. Before they could tell me on the walkie-talkie, I heard Zapater shouting from one of the hospital windows:

" WE'VE GOT HIM!"

Sanchez and that lad, called Luis, had lifted me up and I saw Zapater standing in the window opposite, with both arms raised, yelling, hoarse with triumph:

" SHOT DEAD," he went on screaming. " CAN YOU HEAR ME, SIR?"

It was the least I could do, to hear him. I limped on Sanchez's arm down the stairs and across the street which, by now, had filled with people. Heaven knows where they came from at this late hour. The carabineros were pushing them back, some of them gave me a cheer, but most of them were standing about, as they always do, solemn and hard-faced, as if not the most infamous of all bandits, but one of their own heroes had been killed. This was the time to take their names, to mark the trustworthy against the rebels, now a child could tell a friend of the State from the enemy of the régime.

Zapater came down the stairs and shook my hand, congratulating me.

" A tremendous triumph for you, sir," he said. " I can just imagine how you must feel, hunting him for all these years."

He sounded genuine and my heart filled with warmth. He took my other arm and we went upstairs. Nobody had touched anything before I arrived. The doorways, the upper landing, every corner was crowded with our men and the staff from the hospital. The scene looked ugly, but soldiers, policemen and hospital staff were used to it. The man—human only in his species, not in his behaviour —seemed to me rather disappointingly old and worn.

Perhaps death had something to do with that. The long war
of almost two decades between us had been concluded and
I was the victor. What did Zapater say: A tremendous
triumph. That's what it was. I had not been in on the
kill, but killing is easy—it's the planning that matters. To
outwit, to corner the enemy, this is a general's job. When
I voiced my disappointment, at not being right here when
Artiguez fell, Zapater shook his head.

"Napoleon didn't kill anyone in battle, yet the world
remembers him as one of the greatest fighters."

I looked into his face, but could not discover any mockery
in it.

The men from the Press invaded the place, photo-
graphers, the correspondents of the Madrid papers, and
those from Barcelona who came to report the bull-fighting
season and just happened to be at hand. One of them
suggested that surely I'd be president at this year's corrida,
and I shrugged my shoulders with a smile. If they wanted
me to be president at the bullfights, I wouldn't disappoint
them. No false modesty in me, gentlemen.

The chief surgeon asked if the body should be taken to
the hospital mortuary and I said it should after the police-
photographer and the newspapermen had finished with it.
A Barcelona reporter asked if Manuel Artiguez's mother,
Pilar, would still be in the mortuary? I wanted to know
who told him about her since it was a well-kept secret, and
part of my plan to trap Artiguez, but the reporter just
smiled and wouldn't say more than: "Trade secret!"

So Pilar and Manuel Artiguez, mother and son, were to
meet after all. The Barcelona reporter thought it a good
angle for a story. Personally, I found it rather gruesome.

Shortly after 1.30 a.m., Zapater and I went back to the

policia. My knee felt much better. In my waiting-room a black figure sat on the bench, his head slumped forward, asleep.

" Good heavens!" Zapater said, " Father Francisco."

The priest woke up, succeeded in focusing his eyes and his mind in a remarkably short time, and rose. I asked him to be seated and told him that Artiguez was dead. He stared at me stupefied.

" I'll see you in a moment, Father."

He said nothing, sat down, wide-awake, looking after us as we went into my office.

Zapater asked: " What are we going to do with him?"

I thought it over for a while. This was a most curious business. If Carlos told the truth, this priest had done something outrageous. He was supposed to have unmasked Carlos and warned Manuel Artiguez about my trap. What did this prove? First, it proved that Artiguez did not come to Pamplona in order to see his mother since he knew that Pilar was dead. Why did he come then? Perhaps to take revenge on Carlos. But surely, knowing that the hospital was bristling with our men, he wouldn't have risked going there. He could have found Carlos somewhere else in Pamplona. Just as deadly for Carlos but less risky for himself. Well, let's see what light the father can throw on it. And let's be careful. We don't want to get involved with the clergy if we can avoid it. Understood? Zapater nodded.

Father Francisco came in, wide-eyed, but not frightened. I would have described him as slightly aggressive had it not been for the fact that I was used to frightened people, and those who weren't always impressed me as cocksure. He admitted having met the bandit, Artiguez, he did not deny seeking him out at his home in Pau.

" You actually admit to having acted against the law, Father?"

" Not against *my* law," he said.

" Is there more than one law?"

He thought before he answered. " There shouldn't be. But there is."

" Explain, Father."

" There is the law of God. And there is the law of those who think they *are* gods."

" For instance?"

" That old woman who died, had asked me to save her son. According to my law she was just a mother wishing to help her son. According to your law she was the mother of a bandit. There is only a nuance of difference, but two whole worlds divide them: your world and mine."

" If I put you in the dock, do you think this explanation will save you?"

" I don't. But then I care little to be saved in *your* dock."

" You think His Eminence, the Bishop, would support your views?"

" I wouldn't know. But if he doesn't, he shouldn't be a bishop."

For a second it took me by surprise to hear *that* much independence, *that* much rebellion from a priest.

Zapater spoke up: " Forgive me, sir."

I nodded and he turned to the young priest.

" Father Francisco, if it was the Lord's purpose to save this bandit, why has he been killed?"

The priest's eyes lit up with strange fire. " Oh, but he died of his own accord. The death you planned for him and the death he actually suffered were as different as life and death."

" He died of his own accord?" Zapater asked.

Father Francisco nodded. He spoke gently. " I think so. He didn't have to come here. He knew that his mother was dead."

I broke in. " What made him come then?"

The priest turned to me, waited and then, to my astonishment, started to smile. " I think—he wanted to save me."

There was a long pause. I looked at Zapater and he looked at me. We had the same thought: the man must be mad.

" You see," the priest went on, " he reacted to my coming to warn him exactly the same as you did: he could not believe it. He could not see the purpose in it. I had a long talk with him—we talked through the best part of the night and when it dawned on him that I came because I had to, because I'm a priest who had heard an old woman's last wish, and had to fulfil it, when he grasped that, he felt confused and, yes, I think I'm right in saying, ashamed. A part of his world had tumbled down. He thought that we, priests, were nothing but parasites and liars. For him forgiveness meant nothing but weakness. Suddenly, he began to worry about me, and about his own philosophy of life. He knew that Captain Viñolas would figure out who could have warned Artiguez, the bandit, even if Carlos had not told him. He racked his brain how I could save myself, and when I told him that I wouldn't lie, he got almost desperate. It did not seem right to him that *he* should be saved, that Carlos, the traitor, should escape and I, alone, should be punished. He did not wish to be a lesser man than I was, especially not a lesser man than a priest."

No one spoke. I threw a glance at the clock on the wall. It showed almost 2 a.m. All that the priest had said

sounded strange and dangerous. Still, we had killed
Manuel Artiguez and I, for one, could not think of a
better explanation why he went into my trap. I said:

"Lieutenant Zapater will take you home, Father."

I sighed, and thought: It has taken twenty years to
finish off Manuel Artiguez. But to get the better of the
clergy—you couldn't do it in 20,000 years. This was the
strangest damn' case in my career and one that contained
more dynamite than was needed to blow us all to smither-
eens. So I added: "Don't say a word about it. We'll see
what we can do."

Zapater nodded understandingly. He asked the priest to
wait for him outside, and when we were alone, he said:
"Clear as mud." And I replied: "If he is right, it is he
who should get the reward of 100,000 pesetas."

He laughed and went outside.

Paco slammed the door of my car, the man on guard duty
saluted, Paco climbed behind the wheel and we were off.
On the square he slowed down, opened the glass partition
and asked:

"Where to, sir?"

I thought for a moment as if I had to make a vital
decision.

"It's too late. It would be wrong to wake up the whole
house at home."

"It would, sir," said Paco.

There was no necessity to say more. He took the street
to the left, stopped the car in front of Rosana's house and
rang the bell. He asked what time he should call for me
in the morning, said several times, "Yes, sir," and left as
soon as I got into the house. The porter let me in, stepping
discreetly behind the open door, and staying there, while

I climbed the stairs, so that he could switch on the automatic light in case it went out. He had to press the button three times before Rosana appeared. He was probably thinking what names I would have called *him,* if *he* had let me wait that long. Rosana looked sleepy, her hair tousled, wearing a lacy nightgown. She put her arms around me as soon as we were inside. She really loved me, this girl. No woman can pretend love when just woken up in the dead of night. I told her what had happened. Her first reaction was that we must go to Lourdes together to burn candles to the Holy Virgin. I, for the help received in fulfilling my life ambition, and she for having a brave, famous and generous friend like me. When I told her that I would prefer to go to Biarritz for a few days with her and that from there we could slip over to Lourdes, light as many candles as she wanted, and rush back to Biarritz where I knew a perfect night-club, also with many candles, and a sensational jazz-pianist, she said that I was a favourite of the gods and I was taking advantage of it, and I was a favourite of hers, too, and I took advantage of that also.

She fell asleep in my arms, surrounding me, encircling me with her lazy body, her incompetent legs which were not made for walking, her indolent arms which couldn't do a stroke of work.

I thought that she must be right. Indeed, I *was* a favourite of the gods. Why else did they pile upon me all these favours? Had I not a wife who trusted me? Had I not a mistress who was a true angel? Had I not a wonderful horse, better than I had ever hoped to have? Hadn't I put an end to Manuel Artiguez to-night? Wasn't it wonderful that it had happened to-night, and not ten years ago? If it had, who would remember it now?

Of course, there was a credit side to it. I was always,

I still am and shall remain, a righteous man. I was a dutiful husband, my wife had everything she wanted, I would not force her to travel with me since she hates leaving the house, for any length of time, on account of her skin disease. I shall not prosecute the priest, for he is a fool and fools should be treated gently. I'll give him money, so that he can light some candles on my behalf. A priest knows better than I do how many candles one does light and where and when. I shall sit beside my wife at the bullfights, in spite of her skin disease, so that she can be proud of me. And I shall buy for that girl who had those strong white teeth and eyes like a twin-barrelled gun, but hadn't a decent pair of shoes, or the right sort of skirt, or any long nylon stockings—I shall buy all these things for her. And more.

THE END